UNDONE

UNDONE

THE MURPHY SERIES BOOK 5

HOLLY MORTIMER

Paperback ISBN: 978-0-9952258-5-5

Formatting by Kate Tilton's Author Services, LLC (www.katetilton.com)

For M&L. Don't ask me to pick a favourite.
Love, Mom

CHAPTER ONE

ASHLYN

I grabbed the "Holy Shit" handle as Ox took the turn a hell of a lot faster than was necessary, considering we were driving the Irish back roads in a beat up old Land Rover that had seen better days.

"Jesus," I whispered under my breath.

"He's not going to help you anymore, luv. It's Ox the Fox here with you now."

I rolled my eyes and tried not to feed his ego by laughing at his lame joke. The truth was, he was a fox and built like an ox, but he already knew that and loved spending his time letting me know how many other women agreed.

We both knew it didn't matter what either of us thought. I'd been to Ox Town and thankfully had bought a return ticket. That's what happens when best friends get drunk on a night when they're both sad and lonely and feeling sorry for themselves. They decide to "give it a go" and then, cue the awkward aftereffects. As if a hangover wasn't bad enough. We had to add sex regrets into the mix.

We shook hands, agreed to stay best besties and ran like

hell to our respective homes, only to return to work the next day acting as if nothing had happened.

And here we were, months later still the best of friends, on our way to an urgent callout for a second opinion. You see, Ox was also my employee. Yup, it got that awkward.

I didn't always include Ox in my second opinion calls, but for this one in particular, I needed a seconder, or should I say, thirder?. I often left the McDaniel racing farm vowing revenge of some sort, personally ready to go to war with someone in that godforsaken family.

They didn't call me in all that often for my medical opinion, but when they did, I knew what the score usually was. Their head vet wanted to push the horse through whatever injury it was dealing with and before they did that, they wanted a second vet to agree. Why they continued to ask me to be the seconder, I had zero clues. It was a rare sunny day in Ireland that I agreed with anything they decided on. It had been well over a year since their last call, so this one had taken me by surprise.

"So…" I turned to Ox. "What are you thinking?"

"About?"

I sighed. "Don't be obtuse. It doesn't look good on you."

He glanced at me. "Fancy words, Ash." He swerved to avoid an oncoming Golf clearly unsure of how to drive these narrow roads and most likely a terrified tourist. "I'm thinking they've got no other options for vets and someone up the chain of command has decreed that this horse needs to go. It'll be your job to make sure that happens. Of course, what they've clearly forgotten is that you don't play nice with many people. Well, I'll amend that to, with anyone."

He turned sharply, slamming me into the side of the SUV. I wasn't going to deny his statement. He was right. I struggled to play nice with others. I was terrible at playing politics to close deals, or whatever it was that I was supposed to be doing with the breeding side of my business. It was the reason I had hired Ox to manage my veterinary practice in the first place. He could deliver the worst news possible and make it okay, he could tell the rudest person known to man to fuck off, and they'd thank him for it. I only made things worse when I opened my mouth. No point in denying it.

My job was to heal animals, not people.

"I'm also thinking they're trying to butter you up."

That hit the nerve he had intended it to. McDaniel Farms wanted to buy my farm. The problem was, I wasn't selling. Until last month when my reality had started to sink in. That was when my trusted office manager, Laney, suddenly crossed the floor and went to the dark side. The dark side being the compound we were about to enter. From that day on, the craziest, shittiest stuff had been happening to my farm. Things like horses going missing that were up for inspection. Spooked horses losing their mind and getting hurt, a large part of my records going missing and the big one, my farm's reputation had taken a nose dive. It didn't take a genius to add two plus two and come up with one Laney O'Rourke.

Making matters incredibly worse, Rexford McDaniel the Second had been sending his gooney lawyer over every few days to offer to buy the farm, doing us a "huge favor." I never would have thought I would be in a position to take the offer, but the farm was running on skeleton staff thanks to all the defectors, and my horses were underperforming when being shown. I wasn't an idiot. I knew sustaining a thoroughbred operation was incredibly challenging and expensive. This couldn't go on much longer. I needed to solve the problem, find the constant leak or just give up and sell.

I would have sold long ago, if not for the fact that the farm was my inheritance. Each of the five children in my family were gifted a "piece of Ireland" when my mother passed away years ago. Since I was a vet and loved horses, logically, the ailing family horse operation went to me. I wasn't keeping it because I loved breeding, I was keeping it out of a strong sense of obligation to my Irish roots.

"Well, I guess we'll wait and see what we're dealing with until we play good cop, bad cop."

He slowed the truck and turned down the impressive lane to McDaniel Farms. We followed the drive to the stables, parked and went inside to find the offices.

Up ahead, I could see the operations manager striding towards us. Allan McDaniel was a tall, arrogant asshole of a man and my stomach turned at the site of him. The last time we'd seen each other, he had hovered over me, his stale, hot breath crawled over my neck, making my skin crawl. He had a nasty habit of staring at my breasts and making disgusting remarks towards me whenever I ran into him. This reaction completely pissed me off, as his presence usually took me off my A game and that was never a place I wanted to be. I was a damn good vet and being a female in a male dominated industry, I unfortunately needed to work extra hard to keep my operation on top.

I wiped my sweaty hands on my scrubs and fell back to let Ox greet him. They shook hands and Allan completely ignored me. Another pet peeve of mine and Ox's. The inherent sexism inside this entire operation.

"Thanks for coming on such short notice, Ox."

My eyes rolled back at least 180 degrees at this asshole's idiocy. Ox was firmly on team Murphy. He was the only person I had on staff that I trusted with my life. He was my person, my best friend and he always had my back.

"Excuse me? You called for Doctor Murphy, not her assistant and Doctor Murphy is working on a tight timeline today so give her the respect she deserves. What are we looking at?"

He gently nudged me ahead, falling back like the legit wingman he was. My assistant though? That was new.

We followed Allan down the hallway, marveling at the state-of-the-art large animal hospital we were walking through. I didn't have a surgery on my farm, just a few dedicated treatment rooms. I preferred to work out in the field, where the horse was much more comfortable, but I also knew that had many limitations. Unfortunately, McDaniel's clinic was the closest and simplest option. It hurt hard when I had to come here, but it was incredibly well set up and could serve my needs easily.

They had a couple of vets on staff, so it was rare that I got a call such as this one. I wondered what had happened as we were ushered through the doors at the end of the hall into the recovery area of the facility.

I could see a few people standing around a mare that was clearly distressed and trying not to put any weight on her hind right leg.

"Sadie injured her hind leg yesterday while stretching her legs. We've had our team look at her, but our staff vet has not been responding to our calls and we need to make quick assessment and treatment decisions before the day is out. Sadie is due to breed at the end of the week."

"Well, you're going to have to delay, obviously. I can tell that just standing here and looking at her." Jesus, these guys. The poor thing could hardly bear any weight on her injured leg and they wanted her on the mounting block in three days? Typical men. Dicks. The whole lot of them. My man-hater monologue was moments away from surfacing. Time to get to work.

I ignored them all and cautiously approached Sadie, offering her my hands to inspect, trying desperately not to upset her with my presence. She whinnied and leaned into me while I sent soothing strokes up and down her neck and sides, whispering messages of calm while I slowly probed my way down her body.

I had grown up obsessed with horses, begging and pleading for one of my own nearly every day, until my parents gave in and started with a pony. I had to board the pony at a farm outside the city where we lived, and every day I made the trek with one of my older brothers or a parent to spend as much time as possible caring for Tricky Licky. Hey, I was eight and he licked a lot. How could I not have called him that!

Even at that young age, I could calm a horse with incredible ease. I had quickly earned the nickname, The Horse Whisperer. So original, but it stuck. I rarely spoke to anyone outside my family and even they didn't get much, but horses, they got all of me.

I studied with a singular purpose. To become a vet who specialized in horses and the horse-whisperer nickname had stuck. I heard Ox calling me that to someone behind me as everyone watched me work. That was fine. I was a master at tuning people out. All that mattered to me was Sadie.

"What's going on here?"

I ignored the new player who had just walked in. Whoever he was, he wasn't my concern. American, like me. I could at least tell that from his accent.

I continued on with my thorough inspection of the horse and slowly made my way down until I came within striking distance of the injured area.

I gently probed the muscle surrounding the bone where I suspected she had a fracture and tuned back into the conversation surrounding me.

"Why is there a woman examining Sadie? Where's Tom?"

"She's the local vet. Tom said he wanted a second opinion, we called her, she's here, he's not. No clue where he is actually. Won't take more than another minute, then we can move her."

"She has a name." This voice I recognized. Ox.

"I don't care what her name is, I want her gone from the premises and Tom in here in the next five minutes." That again from the one I didn't know.

Sadie's leg jolted and I settled her again. I didn't think the bone was broken through, but it was still significant enough to have me taking her out of commission and on rest for the short term. At least until they could x-ray her and see what they were dealing with.

I felt Ox squat down beside me as I finished up my examination, and he whispered, "Think it's time we aborted this mission, chief."

"I know. I just need a couple more minutes," I said without looking at him. I could feel his tension radiating from beside me and as I focused on my surroundings once again, the lack of noises above me meant there was more tension happening in the room than I was possibly aware of.

"Miss Murphy. That will be enough, thank you." The masculine voice I'd heard moments ago came from above, his directive was delivered with as much derision and authority as I'd expected from someone in their organization.

I'd had enough and was gladly open to leaving. As long as I got my two cents in first. Popping up with Ox, I turned to find the body that went with the voice was much closer than I had anticipated. Not one to ever back down from a challenge, and not being a tiny woman, I didn't move an inch and stared back into the most arresting blue eyes I thought I'd ever seen.

But man, were they attached to the most arrogant face I thought I'd also ever encountered. Incredible, long, thick and wavy dirty-blonde hair framed a rugged, scruff-covered face. A face that wasn't giving me that inch I wanted.

He raised a single, gloriously wild eyebrow at me and I smirked my signature Murphy smirk. "It's Doctor Murphy. And you are?"

His hands were shoved into his jeans' pockets and the navy blazer he wore was stretched tight over his incredibly broad shoulders. No doubt he had acquired said shoulders in the gym, while admiring himself and his lovely locks in the mirror.

The arrogant asshole wasn't going to answer me and our staring match was most likely making our audience uncomfortable. I heard some throat clearing and foot shifting going on around us but was struggling to care.

"Whatever." I shook my head and tried to ignore the weird energy running through me. "Since I was called here to offer my medical opinion, I'll give it and then gladly vacate the premises. Sadie appears to have a fractured cannon bone. She'll need to be taken off whatever rotation you have her on, X-rays done to determine the depth of the break and then rest until it heals completely. I'm thinking you'd be looking at at least three to four weeks without her."

He tilted his head slightly and his hair fell over his shoulder. Why did men with long hair always have the best hair? It was truly tragic looking at his gentle curls, and probably unnaturally blonde streaked hair.

He removed one hand from his pocket and stroked his beard while continuing our impromptu staring contest.

I mimicked his single brow raise and not for the first time since I had stepped onto McDaniel soil, wondered what the hell I was playing at here? I'd have typically let him have the piece of my mind I rarely kept locked up and then been halfway home by now. Instead, I was here playing eyebrow chicken with the arrogant bastard, who by the way, had toed himself forward when I wasn't paying attention, staying completely stuck in his weird tractor beam eyes.

8

"Thanks, sweetheart. We'll take it from here."

Oh he did not just call me sweetheart. "You—"

Ox grabbed my elbow and pulled me away before I Mortal-Combatted Fabio. "Let's go Ash. Not worth it."

"Listen to your boyfriend, Doctor Murphy. Make sure reception has your contact information so we can pay you for your services, but we won't be needing you anymore."

"Jesus Christ, you arrogant ass—"

I felt another tug on my arm and I was quickly being propelled forward by Ox. I shrugged him off and turned on my heel. I pointed to the poor, injured horse I had sworn to protect during my vet oath-taking and let him have the very last piece of my mind I was going to waste on him.

"I don't know who you are, but clearly, you think you're many, many things. Please consider removing Sadie from your racing or breeding rotation and give the poor thing some rest, otherwise you'll run the danger of doing permanent damage. And now I'm leaving and really hope that you call another vet the next time you need a second opinion. I'd rather die a thousand fiery deaths than come near your egotistical ass again."

Said asshole strode around the horse to restart our toe-to-toe stare down and I rolled my eyes. God save me from men who needed to have the last word.

"My name is Rexford McDaniel, Doctor Murphy. Our farms share a perimeter fence. I'm sure this isn't the last time you'll be seeing my egotistical, incredible ass. I truly look forward to our next meeting...sweetheart."

I would not rise to his bait. I would not rise to his bait. No, I needed to put that shit on repeat and walk away with my dignity.

I sent my fingernails into my palms, pivoted on my heel and stormed ahead of Ox. I slammed through the door to the reception area, still feeling that intense stare behind me, but I refused to acknowledge him any longer.

Still fuming, I got into Ox's truck, slammed the door and silently sulked while he got in.

"Jesus, Mary and Joseph, Ash. What was that little display in there?"

"Seriously? That dickwad started it."

"Oh, are we back in primary school, then?" He navigated the truck down the drive and out onto the road where I finally breathed a sigh of relief to be away from that crazy place.

"You saw him. He was an egotistical, modern day Fabio. Someone needed to show him he wasn't all that and a slice of toast."

He just smiled at the road ahead. His lack of support was making me madder and I knew somehow, at some point, I had decided I was spoiling for a fight. It only made me angrier when I couldn't find one and Ox knew me well enough to know that.

He burst out laughing and I slumped in my seat, arms crossed, bottom lip all the way out. It was official. I was pathetic. Something needed to break in my life. Everyone around me was so freaking happy and it only irritated me more.

Even my miserable brother Quinn had found happiness. And of course, he had stolen my best friend Violet in order to accomplish it. Even though they lived down the road from me, I still didn't see her as often as I wanted.

It was official, I had flown by pathetic and landed wherever the hell the next stop was. I was lonely. I had no friends who didn't work for me—or weren't biologically attached to me somehow. No boyfriend, no dating prospects, and I hadn't gotten laid in who the hell knew how long? I was probably able to be reclassified as a born-again virgin at this point.

"Are you needing the violin again, Ash? Get your head out of your rear, girl."

I gave Ox my long-perfected stink eye, hoping he would receive the message loud and clear.

"You know what you need?" He looked at me with his usual lopsided grin. I just stared back at him, already knowing the gist of what he was going to come back at me with.

"Okay, gonna be that way then, I see. Why yes Oxford O'Connor, please, do tell me what it is I need, since you've always been spot on with all of your advice."

I cracked a smile and dug deep to keep the full-on smile at bay. Feeding his fire wasn't a wise decision for me today. I just wanted to get back to the farm and forget about the McDaniels for the foreseeable future.

"You need to get laid."

"Jesus, Ox. Come on."

"No one else seems to be telling you, so leave it to your buddy Ox. You need a good shag, love. Stat. Before you forget how."

I threw my head back and laughed. Of course he wasn't telling me anything I didn't already know. "Oh, Ox," I hung my head in my hands. "What am I gonna do?"

"Are you finally asking me for my help, Ash? 'Cause God knows, I've been waiting for this moment for going on a year or so now. Sweet Jesus, as your best friend, I volunteer. Choose me as tribute. I'll have you right sorted out by tomorrow."

I went back to glaring at him. "No! Ox, that is not what I'm saying. We've been there, done that, remember? Please, I do not need your assistance."

"Well then, who are you calling in? You know if you don't commit, it's not gonna happen. Tell me now, who is it?"

The idea of creating a project "Get Ash Laid" for my sisters was percolating inside of me, and fortunately, I had one sister who happened to be my ace in the hole.

"Sam."

He hooted and slammed his hand on the steering wheel. "This, Ashlyn Marie Murphy, is going to be fucking incredible. You do know your sister-in-law has been waiting for this job vacancy to open up for quite some time, right?"

Oh I knew. Sam was actually my sister-in-law. She was married to my oldest brother, Brennan. But she also happened to be an incredibly beautiful and very famous actress who also happened to now be based here in Ireland, raising their three children. She'd been without a project for quite some time, and I knew she was chomping at the bit to pull me kicking and screaming into her world.

Today was just a reminder of how much I needed her. Even though Rexford McDaniel had treated me like dirt, and even though his long hair offended all my sensible tendencies, I couldn't get the jerk and his glorious blue eyes out of my head, and every time I closed my eyes I smelled his spicy scent, and my traitorous lady bits tried to claw their way back to life.

If I was going to survive the dating wilds, I needed Sam, stat.

CHAPTER TWO

REX

*T*hings had just gotten complicated. I watched her walk away from where I stood, hands in fists and visibly enraged. God, she was incredible. I'd heard of the illustrious Doctor Murphy, but was woefully unprepared for the real thing.

An Amazonian warrior queen would be an apt description for her and all the more reason for me to stay the fuck away. The last thing I needed in my life right now was another complication. This farm was enough to send me spinning and looking for inner peace for the majority of the day, each and every day.

My father sure had outdone himself this time. His latest throwdown for me was the last place I had ever thought I'd finally give in to him. He'd been sending me on his little missions for my entire life. Testing me. Always holding the carrot just out of reach, until the carrot just disappeared for a while.

I was Rexford Magnus McDaniel III, and the old fucker had never let me forget how I had failed to live up to the ridiculous name he had forced my mother to give me. What I couldn't understand was how long I was going to run myself into the ground trying to become anything other than a disappointment to him.

The latest test he'd given me? Make Doctor Ashlyn Murphy sell him her horse farm, the land included, and grow the McDaniel Farm and Breeding Facility to become the largest in the country and ranked among the top in the world. It was a tall order and the land purchase part was a dick move, but that wasn't anything new. Based on the minimal research I'd been doing, I knew the land was gifted to her from her mother and father when they had passed and the buildings on the property were owned by her as well. The two neighboring homes were owned by two of her three brothers. Family businesses made for difficult purchases and I had no idea, if I was being honest with myself, how I was going to accomplish this one without losing the very tiny scrap of my soul I had managed to keep hidden from my father.

I turned to my staff and carefully schooled my face into a neutral zone, leaving the smile behind. God, I hated that prick, Allan. The look on his smug-assed face was one I was working on figuring out how to wipe off. But for now, I had to play nice with everyone in this room, Allan included.

"Someone want to tell me what happened to the vet we had on staff? Why in the hell did we have to pull Doctor Murphy in?"

Allan stepped forward, always the eager beaver when it came to throwing others under the proverbial bus. "Mr. McDaniel, he has quit."

"Quit. Why?" Great, just what I needed.

Allan was looking anywhere but directly at me, a quality I absolutely hated. "Well, I'm not—"

"He said he couldn't work for this soul-sucking place a

minute longer, sir." This from a new voice I hadn't heard before. A tiny, red-headed female popped out from behind one of the men lingering about.

"And you are?" God, I sounded like a supreme asshole. She was right of course, this place was soul-sucking. It was unfortunate I couldn't really agree with her in front of these guys.

"Laney, sir." She was a tiny thing, and didn't look old enough to be here during the day, in the middle of the school year.

"Rexford—" Allan started.

I glared at him, daring him to say anything else. The slimy bastard squirmed, looking, again, anywhere but at the man challenging him. "Laney, feel like a walk?"

The color of Allan's face was worth getting out of bed today to deal with this shit.

"Sure!"

I turned to look at Allan as we walked away. "Sadie's off for whatever it is you had set up for her this week and next. Get the good Doctor Murphy back here in 48 hours. I don't care what you have to do to get her here, just do it. And have the X-rays and follow-up tests complete before she sets foot on this property again. She can examine them and decide our course of action for Sadie."

Allan's mouth opened and closed about sixteen times while he processed all the words I'd just thrown at him. I knew damn well none of those things were his responsibility, but damn, it was fun watching him flounder.

"Sir—"

"Oh, and Allan?" Just one last jab to fuck with him.

He just looked at me, trying to contain the rage. Priceless. "Yes?"

"Have four new vets lined up for me to interview by the end of the week."

"But—"

I turned to Laney, finding her desperately trying, and failing, to hide a smile. I guess Allan wasn't well liked by more than just me and the doctor. "So, Laney. Tell me more about this soul-sucking work environment."

CHAPTER THREE

ASHLYN

"*This* was a mistake." I was trying to escape the clutches of my uber evil sister and sisters-in-law and failing miserably. I wasn't fast enough. Violet held me in place by my shoulders, turned me back around and pushed me down into the chair I had so recently vacated.

"Sit." She was officially off my Christmas list. Now that she was my ex best friend and all that.

"What are we even doing? This mission is doomed. Look at me. I look like a hooker. And a cheap one at that."

"Maybe," Sam said. "But, you're wrong. You're like a super high-class hooker! More Julia Roberts after Richard Gere transformed her, not before."

This was such a bad idea. Why did I let Ox talk me into it? The very last thing I needed was to veer from the course that I had set out for myself. Graduate vet college. Use my inheritance to renovate the barns and grow my breeding and vet business so I could build a second barn and convert the oldest one into my living quarters. Then grow the business more and become a crazy horse recluse lady. The plan was a good one. There was no need to deviate from it.

Finding a man wasn't in the plan. I'd never been a sexual being, I was just shit at it. I must have been away the day they handed out sex skills. I was completely uncomfortable with myself. Just under six feet tall, built like a "brick house," as my last date had said. Long, boring black hair. Plain face. I wasn't in possession of any sort of milkshake and there were zero boys coming to my yard growing up. I struggled to find a reason to even try.

All of my sexual experiences had been completely uneventful. For me anyway. That's right. I was still searching for that elusive "O" during sex.

Oh, I was in possession of my trusty sidekick, Virginia the virginal vibrator. That's what my baby sister Keeva had nicknamed my vibrator after way too many beers one night.

"Stop, Ash. Do not even start that shit that I can see running through your gigantic brain right now." Sam dug her fingers into my hair, shook everything up and then reversed everything she had just done by smoothing it all down.

"I'm hopeless. Why are we even trying? I don't know how to talk to men. I'm either completely nerdy or completely bitchy. I have zero middle ground." I emphasized my point by crossing my arms over my chest and pulling a pout.

Sam, having zero personal boundaries, reached into my arms and pulled my boobs up and over. "There. That's better. Lead with the girls, Ash. Always the girls. Men struggle to see past them."

"One hundred percent. Boobs in. But not too far in," Violet added. "Too far in and you look whoreish. Just let your boobs do the walking and the talking."

I buried my head in my hands and prayed for patience. "Guys!"

Sam swung me around and crouched down in front of me. Violet came around to stand beside her and I knew they'd had enough and I was in for an ass kicking.

"Ashlyn Marie Murphy. Your brother has no idea what I'm doing here," Sam said. "And if he did, he'd withhold sex from me for at least three days, the bastard. I'm risking everything by being here."

"Everything? That's a little dramatic, isn't it? Three days without sex is no big deal."

"Shut up. I'm talking. And yes, your brother is very good with his special talents. Three days is an eternity."

"Please." I held up a hand. "Please, do not go on."

She glared at me and I was face-to-face with the version of Sam no one, and I mean no one, wanted to be near, let alone on the receiving end of.

"Ash, you will listen to me. You are marching into your room. You will put on the outfit I secretly stashed and brought here, unbeknownst to your brother. You will let us finish your hair and touch up the makeup you messed up with your tantrum. You will walk into the bar we have purposely chosen far, far away from Murphys and you will give this mission all of your attention and efforts."

The door opened and my baby sister Keeva flew in, her husband Nixon following behind her, balancing a pile of groceries and other bags.

"I've got the goods, sisters of mine," she announced to the room. She pulled up short when she looked at me and bent over, busting a gut laughing. "Shit, Ash. My street corner is already taken. We're going to have to move a little farther out so you don't start a hooker turf war."

"See! I told you guys!" I was so done. I couldn't leave her house like this and I hadn't even gotten to the non-existent scrap of fabric they called a dress.

"Keeva!" Sam used her mommy voice. It worked on most people, adults and children alike, but she'd met her match with Keev. She was a Murphy and the most like Brennan, our oldest sibling and Sam's husband. She had some sort of immunity to Sam's rants.

"Sam!"

"Okay, ladies. I'm out of here." Nixon, Keeva's husband, was the most grounded and calm of all of us. He had to be, if he was going to hitch his wagon to Keeva's for the rest of his life.

"Bye, babe," he whispered to his wife. I tried not to stare, but my heart hurt watching them. Keeva truly deserved all that was Nixon Rivers. Watching them, I couldn't help but wonder why I'd never met anyone who looked at me the way he looked at her. Like she was his sun and moon and stars. He always had, even from the beginning. It had just taken her a while to see it.

He was cradling her face in his hands, gently kissing her and I knew. I knew it would never be that way for me.

"Close your mouth, Ash. Flies are getting in," Sam whispered in my ear.

"Sam—" I started to say.

"I know, sweetheart. Your turn is out there somewhere." She tucked a stray piece of hair that must have escaped the hairspray she'd lacquered on earlier. She tamed it into submission and smiled at me.

"No, he's not. Look at them. He's big and strong, and she's tiny and full of life. That's never going to happen for me. I'm tall and awkward and refuse to let anyone try to be my protector." I turned away from them, not willing to let anyone else see the deep, dark pain that lived inside me. My family was way too observant and if I let them see how much I really did long to have someone in my life, this night would become next level in a heartbeat.

"Ashlyn Murphy, give your head a shake. What nonsense are you spouting off now?" Violet yelled at me. "Do not cry, I will murder you. That makeup took forever."

I threw my hands down in frustration. "That's just it, Vi. Look at me. Look at how much makeup it took to make me look like something other than a tomboy."

I risked my life and sniffled, trying desperately not to fall apart from being so overwhelmed. The facts were literally staring me in the face. I was too tall, too curvy, too uninterested in much of anything other than my horses. I was out of my element, in an entirely different solar system, and it was messing with my confidence.

Three heads suddenly popped into my blurring vision, surrounding me with their love. "Guys, what if I can't do this? I'm going to be a crazy horse lady soon."

"Too late," Keeva said, laughing. She grabbed my shoulders and gave me a good shake. "Ash, enough. This isn't you, this is all those years of you taking care of everyone else, of being the strong one, of your inability to ask for what you need. You can do this. It's just a night out. Millions of women do it all the time. We've got you." She ended her unusual pep talk with a second shake of my shoulders and Violet came into view.

"Where's Nixon?" I belatedly forgot about my brother-in-law. The poor guy was used to the Murphy women, but still, I wasn't a crier. I also wasn't a girly girl, so perhaps getting all of those shockers out of the way now was good for him. He must have slipped out without saying goodbye.

"Are you shitting me? Four Murphy women rallying? He's probably halfway to the pub by now. He's staying with Bren. I figured the babysitting would do him good, what with the impending joy coming and all."

"Keeva Rivers! Were you just going to not tell us you're pregnant?" I smacked her arm then pulled her in for a bone crushing hug. She was my opposite in every way, especially size. Tiny as I was tall. But, damn she was our baby sister and was having a baby.

21

"It's new, but yes, we're having a baby. Can you believe it? Me! Crazy, irresponsible Keeva Murphy will now be in charge of a tiny human!" She was absolutely glowing. How could I have missed it? Was I so wrapped up in my own misery that I hadn't noticed?

Sam and Violet proceeded to swallow her whole while I heaved out another huge sigh. Keeva was my last hold on feeling normal in this family of extroverts who were in the parental way. We were the last non-parents left in our clan. I was now the odd man out again. The one who was different than all my siblings.

The Murphys were notorious loudmouthed extroverts who loved hearing themselves talk. I didn't talk until I was five. My parents had me at every doctor they could find, did all the exercises they were supposed to, but I refused to give it up. And it had stuck. I was incredibly uncomfortable around strangers, taking forever to warm up. Unless, of course, we were talking about horses. Then I rarely shut up. It made meeting guys kind of hard. And we were back to tonight and the fact that my sisters expected me to talk to men. I started scratching at the imaginary hives I suddenly had all over my arms.

"Stop scratching. Get a hold of yourself, Ash." Sam came over to me. "Let's get you dressed"

I scowled. "Thanks, Mom."

She smiled. No one could give her a better compliment. My sarcasm had fallen on deaf ears. "That's right. Listen to momma and you might just end the night having enjoyed yourself."

"My walls aren't soundproofed," Keeva interjected. "So, keep it down tonight when you bring your hotty home."

"Jesus, Keeva. Baby steps." Sam glared at her.

"Just sayin'."

"What are you 'just sayin'?" Sam asked.

"Just that, well, she needs to get laid, and tonight, if that happens, 'cause God knows it needs to, I'm pregnant and need my rest. So, keep it down!"

"I can't do this." I hopped up and ran into the spare room, trying to escape my insane sisters and their well-meaning, but unwelcome intentions. I immediately heard a soft knock and gave up. They were relentless.

"Ash." Violet softly closed the door. Violet had been my other half since we were children. The best friend who got me, and who I got back and who's also unfortunately now happily married to my obnoxious brother, Quinn. Happily, but still, I missed her like I didn't know I would. They lived a field away from me, but it might as well have been across the country. They had twin daughters and ran a successful baking business in town. Her time for me had dropped off considerably and I should have been doing everything I could to take advantage of this rare night out with her, but instead, I sat paralyzed inside my sister's spare room.

"I can't do this, Vi. This isn't me." I flopped down onto the bed. "I'm Ashlyn Murphy. Tomboy, farm girl, extreme introvert. The end."

She sat down beside me and bumped my shoulder with hers. "Yup, all of those things are very true. But do you know what else you are?"

I rolled my eyes and got ready for one of her famous pep talks. Positivity was Violet's love language and I was about to receive her gift.

"Well, since you're buying into the story you tell yourself over and over, I'll help you get out of your head here."

"I'm—"

"Nope, girl, it's my turn to talk, you just listen. Here's what I see, and what pretty much anyone else you know if you'd just ask. I see a tall, sexy woman."

"Bu—"

"I said listen. That black hair of yours is long, and naturally incredible. Your brain is enormous and it must hurt to carry that thing around every day, but darn it, you're so super smart. You can talk anyone under the table with all that knowledge. Your sarcastic tongue can for sure get you in trouble, but man, it goes down fighting and there have been many, many days I've wished for your brain and sarcastic sense of humor, instead of this sunshiny bullshit that always comes out of my mouth."

I smiled. She was annoyingly happy and positive all the time. This used to drive me nuts in high school, but now, I wished I could have my own dose of the happy sometimes.

Sam opened the door and slid in with a now-silent Keeva.

"Come here." She grabbed my hand and yanked me up off my perch and over to the full-length mirror.

"No." I pulled back. "Sam, please, this isn't necessary."

"Stand up straight. It's time you saw what we all see." She squared my shoulders, practically disappearing behind my giant body. She was the tiny redheaded fairy in our family. She and Keeva were the practically twins, except Vi was the good twin and Keeva was, well, Keeva.

I stood there in my T-shirt and undies and tried to listen to her advice. I tried to see what she saw, but years of beating myself up for all of my problem areas was hard to erase in an instant.

"Tits for days." She hauled up my boobs and gave them a good squeeze. "Stop making that face. People pay good money for girls like these." She grabbed my waist and turned me to the side. "Rear end a man could eat off of. Seriously, this ass is the stuff of Kardashian fame."

"Sam," I whined. "Stop."

Ignoring me, she whipped me back to facing off against myself in the mirror. "This hair, please. Raven black, long, perfect for holding on to." She smirked and raised a single eyebrow and I closed my eyes and tried to just hang on to my sanity. "Open your eyes, Ash. You're going to start seeing what everyone else sees. Time's up. You're not hiding anymore."

I took a deep breath in and slowly let it out. She wouldn't back down and if I wanted this night to end, I was going to have to get it to start. I opened my eyes and did my best to beat down years of negative self-talk. All the self-help books I'd read told me to look in the mirror and find the things I loved about myself. I turned my head back towards the mirror and tried to see what they saw.

Okay, Sam was right. I had good boobs and in this crazy push up bra underneath my T-shirt, they were sitting loud and proud. So proud that they'd be leading me into the bar tonight just as I'd been advised to do. Check.

"Yes, she's seeing it now," Violet said from the bed. She threw my dress at my head. "Put it on. Let's move this forward."

The dress they got me to buy this morning was doing everything they promised, it was true. My legs were my best feature. I was tall and it'd taken me a lot of years to try to learn to come to terms with that. I'd also heard rumors men liked long legs and this dress didn't leave anything to the imagination when it came to the two sticks supporting me.

"How do you even move in a dress like this? One slip up and the wrong cheeks will be hanging out for everyone to see."

"Enough," Sam decried. "You're ready. You're a smart girl, you'll figure it out." She handed me my shoes and I hesitated. The three-inch heels made me over six feet and it wasn't often I found the confidence to own that.

"Put them on and let's head out." She turned me again to face her. "Ash, you can do this. It's just a night out, nothing else. You deserve it. Let's go have some fun. God knows I need a night away from your brother. If nothing else, you owe me that!"

I rolled my eyes, 'cause she wasn't wrong. My oldest brother, Brennan, could be an overbearing dick. Wait, not could...was. I toddled into the living room, held my hand up trying to stave off their comments on my inability to walk in both the shoes and the dress, praying everything stayed in place and prepared myself to drink enough to gain the confidence to emerge from the cocoon I'd been hiding in all my life.

CHAPTER FOUR

REX

"Tell me again why we're doing this at a bar? A dance bar to boot."

"'Cause. You're a bloody bore and it's time you let loose for a change."

"It's called parenting, asshole. Being present with my child is pretty much the only thing being a parent entails."

"Yeah, yeah. You're a martyr for the cause. I get it. Just because your bitch of an ex left you high and dry with the little one, doesn't mean your social life had to end."

I shook my head. Jack's never gotten it. He might have been my father's business manager and the person I spent the most amount of time with outside of my daughter, Miller, but he really was an idiot. One day he might figure it out, but for now, I was stuck in this bar in Galway hoping Mills was listening to her babysitter and not eating every sugary item I had stashed in my secret hiding spots that, I'd discovered, actually weren't so secret.

"Let's just get this meeting done. What's so important it can't wait until Monday?"

He started to tell me about a deal he was interested in and

I immediately lost interest. Jack loved to talk, if only to hear himself talk. Me? I was more of an action kind of guy. I'd only been in Ireland a few months. My father had summoned me here to try once more to mold me to his ways, something if not for Miller, I would have ignored.

Jack droned on about some new project he wanted my dad to undertake when I saw her. Fucking hard not to. She towered above everyone else in the place, but that's not what held my eyes on her. She'd transformed into something I wasn't expecting. I loved things that turned my expectations on their head. Yeah, I'd only met her a couple of days ago and only for a short period of time, but damn, she was unforgettable, and it was the most pleasant surprise to find the esteemed and uptight doctor having transformed my view of her. By the look on her face, she was just as surprised by who she was tonight as me.

Her incredible black hair fell in soft waves down to the middle of her back, begging someone to run their fingers through it and give it a gentle, commanding tug. She wore a dress that molded to her body, hugging every sinful curve as though it was just another layer of her skin.

The sea of people parted between us and I got a clear view of the rest of her. Fuck, those legs. It was so cliché, but they went on and on, ending in heels that only served the rest of her up on a fucking platter.

I finally made it back up to her breasts and my breath caught. They were cleverly hidden beneath her scrubs the last time we met. "Son of a bitch," I whispered under my breath. She was spectacular.

"Rex. Rex, are you even listening to me?" I saw Jack waving his hand in front of my eyes, but the only thing I was currently interested in seeing was Doctor Ashlyn Murphy. "Who in the hell are you looking at?"

I shook myself out of my stupor and reminded myself she

saw me as enemy number one. She wasn't far off on that assessment, but it was my father who was actually enemy number one. I was just another casualty in the endless games he always played. What that made her to me, I wasn't entirely sure, but those complications couldn't keep growing for me. I needed her land to get my dad off my back so I could live here in peace with Miller. My father'd been griping for too long about my lack of abilities when it came to the family business. Turned out, he was mostly right. When I landed here, I was frustrated, and had no idea what this summons would bring. And having a six-year old to raise only served to double the frustration and anxiety.

My ex, having decided she enjoyed pretty much anything other than being a mother, made the unilateral decision to leave Miller and me when she was only a baby. Of course, she thought marrying me would lead her to the top of her social climbing ladder. Too bad she found out pretty quickly I was a huge disappointment to dear old dad and hadn't yet been given free rein to design my own destiny, or access much of my bank account.

I'd been running father dearest's US operations. But one incredibly bad decision, one incredibly devious woman, and the US division CEO position was mine no more. There were no second chances in McDaniel Inc.

Miller's mother had the unique talent of sleeping with the enemy just to gain favors and climb social ladders. When she showed her true colors after I told her I earned a salary just any other normal person and wouldn't see a dime of my inheritance until dear old dad deemed me ready, she decided that divorcing me and latching on to some other unsuspecting man was her next step, and having decided I was unable to run the company without the traditional wife on my arm, dad decided to bring me across the pond to Ireland. Of course, Miller and I were a package deal, something dad couldn't understand. Mothers raised children in his world. It was just one more thing I'd done that was a disappointment in his eyes. I couldn't even choose a proper wife as far as he was concerned.

He tolerated my daughter, but he certainly wasn't going to win grandfather of the year anytime soon. I was now the Vice-President of McDaniel Farms, and was being forced and blackmailed into turning the sinking ship that was the thoroughbred business around. I'd been making inroads fairly well until he had demanded I speed up the growth a few weeks ago, with the edict I snap up the surrounding land using whatever methods it took, and expand the stock.

"Well, she's a tasty little number, isn't she? Haven't seen her around here before." God, he really was disgusting.

"Jack, can we just get this over with. What is it you desperately needed to talk to me about?"

"Fine." He ran off some bullshit directives my father had sent down. I was only partially listening again, trying to keep my eye on Ashlyn as she moved through the bar, barely avoiding a multitude of grabby hands. She had made her way to the bar with the women she was with, shoving their way in to order a round of shots.

I watched her throw back her head and swallow the liquid down, wondering what it would feel like to have that neck under my lips. She pounded the shot glass down on the bar and signaled for another. Looks like Doctor Murphy was looking to get plastered on her girls' night out.

I halfheartedly continued to listen to Jack as he ran down another new deal my father wanted us to be working on next week as she continued on her quest to obliterate her liver. Shot after shot until she suddenly smiled widely and her posse did as girl posses are want to do—collapsed in on each other, laughing at their secret inside joke, making every man within striking distance wishing they were in on it.

I tracked her onto the dance floor like the creeper I'd apparently become, where she proceeded to attract every man, straight or not, to her as she moved to the beat, clearly gifted with some sense of rhythm. My dick stirred and I shifted, not sure how to handle the growing complication that was my attraction to the same woman I was supposed to be "taking down." My father's words, not mine.

I heard voices and realized Jack's abandoned our work conversation and was now talking to two women. Without caring about the so-called complications, because I was nothing if not consistent when it came to diving into complicated situations, I got up and head for the dance floor. Which happened to be a place I hadn't graced in quite some time.

Fighting the rising tide that was surrounding Ashlyn and the women she was with, I wondered what the hell I was playing at. I was supposed to be playing the role of Gigantic Dickhead number one, not Interested Guy Number Ten. Still, I found myself walking up behind her, close enough to catch her scent, which had always been my thing. Shit, I was in so much trouble. I was picking up some sort of earthy scent that immediately had me leaning in for something more.

Feeling me, she spun around and lost her balance, which in turn made her fall right into my arms. I grabbed her by the waist as recognition flared in her eyes. "Well Doctor Murphy. Falling into my arms already, I see."

She raised a single eyebrow and gave me an amused look. Not many women could look me in the eye. At six foot two, it was rare, if ever, that I met a woman who was my match in height. But the beauty standing before me had no problem looking me directly in the eyes. She wore heels, that put her damn close to my height.

"Rexford McDaniel the Third," she drunk yelled. "The absolute last person on earth I wanted to run into tonight."

31

She let out a high pitched giggle, looked disgusted with herself, and then giggled again. Fucking adorable. I was walking a very thin line and she was close to dragging me over it.

I grabbed hold of one of her hands, moving my other hand around her waist to rest on the small of her back. Moving her back and forth to the underlying slow beat of the song, I watched the small changes she allowed her face to reveal. I sent up a silent prayer for all the shots she'd had before this. I had been expecting her to immediately haul off and smack me for the dickheadedness I'd displayed earlier today. I know I sure would have.

"Why's that?"

She slowly smiled as I pulled her just a little bit closer. "This hair of yours…" She ran her fingers through my hair, hair I'd been growing in defiance of my father for quite some time.

"Yes, I have hair. What about it?"

"It's so…" She sighed and I realized she was a little more in her cups than I had originally thought. "Wonderful."

"Wonderful." I smiled back at how adorable she was and tried to remember why I shouldn't have kept dancing with her. Those aforementioned complications were drifting farther away with each sway of our bodies. "I've never quite heard it described like that before."

"Well, it is, you know. Wonderful. And long. Yes, very, very long for a man. I don't like men with better hair than me. It's not right. They're usually way more into their hair than they are me."

"Well then, they're idiots. The lot of them. The only reason I have this hair is to piss off my father."

"Ah." She softly hiccupped. "Daddy issues."

"Something like that."

She paused, chewing on the corner of her bottom lip and damned if my dick didn't stir at the image. "But…"

"But?"

"But the rest of you isn't so wonderful."

"Is that so?" I found myself smiling harder, having a feeling I knew what was coming.

She suddenly rested her head on my shoulder and I wrapped my arm fully around her waist. I saw her friends giving me the sister side-eye and knew I was on borrowed time.

"You were such a jerk to me today, Rexford McDaniel the Third. All I was doing was trying to help when that moron Allan called me in."

"I know babe. I'm sorry." I really was. But that didn't change the fact before the night was through, I'd need to guarantee she hated me again. I had no alternative other than to make her sell me her land. There were so many things that depended on it.

She lifted her head and looked me in the eye, searching for something I wasn't sure I wanted found. "You are?" She tilted her head to the side and chewed her bottom lip. "You called me babe. That's nice. Totally alpha of you, but nice."

I chuckled and noticed her friends closing in on us and that meant my time was nearly up. "I did and I am. I was, well still am, dealing with some details that unfortunately you and I aren't ever going to see eye to eye on."

She rested her head again on my shoulder and I inhaled her intoxicating scent. "My farm."

"Let's make a deal, shall we?"

"I don't want to," she mumbled into my shoulder. God, adorable. "Your deal isn't good for me."

"Oh but I disagree. This deal I think you'll like, Doctor Murphy." Where in the hell I was taking this was beyond my comprehension, but I couldn't stop myself. Once I had her in my arms, I was terribly reluctant to let her go.

"Okay, what's this big deal?" She nestled in deeper.

"Look at me, Doctor Murphy."

She lifted her head and raised both eyebrows. "That's very formal, Mr. McDaniel." The way she drew my name out, letting each syllable roll slowly off her tongue, had the naughty bugger in my pants itching to get out.

"Go out on a date with me." Shit, where in the hell had that come from? Complications. Her eyes widened and she tilted dangerously to the right.

She looked at me, attempted to raise one eyebrow but failed miserably and just ended up looking insane. "No deal. Dating you is a very, very, very bad idea."

Sick bastard that I was, I felt a little angry at her logical stance on the subject. Even though I well knew dating her could never, ever happen. I needed her farm, she needed to keep me away from her farm. It was simple, really. We couldn't become anything other than business associates. But still, I stayed where I was, anticipating her reaction.

"Wow, three verys. That seems quite final."

We started swaying again gently to the beat of the music and I held her just a tiny bit tighter, seeing the end to our truce coming quickly. I wasn't an idiot. I was well aware the only reason I got this close was thanks to the copious amounts of alcohol Ashlyn had consumed. Even though we'd only met once before, I could easily see the woman in my arms wasn't one that would ever let someone push her around.

She poked a long, elegant finger into my chest, and my dick twitched again. "It is. Final. Very much so."

I grabbed a hold of that delectable finger and slowly raised it to my mouth, where I placed it against my lips. I watched her eyes flare and her cheeks flush even more than the alcohol was already accomplishing. Closing my eyes, I very much wished we were two different people, with two different circumstances. I didn't have the ability to pursue anything with the alluring Doctor Murphy. My responsibilities were too great and she deserved so much more than what I could offer her.

"No, you're right, Doctor. It is very much a bad idea, and still, I'm reluctant to let you go without at least the taste of the promise of what could have been."

She was standing still now, a mesmerized look on her face as I still held her solitary finger to my mouth. Taking a hold of her entire hand, I moved it out of my way, leaning down only slightly as this tall, incredible creature nearly matched me in height, and softly brushed my lips across hers.

CHAPTER FIVE

ASHLYN

I was drunk, that I'll easily admit to. But I wasn't so far gone that I could blame what I was feeling on anything other than that great unexplainable thing that happens when someone plants one on you that changes things. Rexford McDaniel had just changed things and I didn't know what to do about it. The night had turned out to be surprisingly fun and I was dangerously close to letting something else happen with him.

Close, but not that far gone. And so, now I had a choice. He wanted a date. He also wanted my farm. The two weren't compatible pathways. He was the enemy. Dating the enemy had been proven to be a very bad idea in every drama I'd ever watched on Netflix. However, every incredible romance novel I'd read, dating the enemy turned out to be quite hot and very fruitful when it came to enemy sex.

Of course, I was smart enough to know that this wasn't a Hallmark holiday movie, but drunk enough to possibly not care. So, I was back to the choice that I needed to make.

I knew deep down what that choice was but damn it, for once I wanted to be irresponsible Ashlyn. Not a vet, not a business owner, but a carefree thirty-five-year-old who was interested in taking this incredible male specimen home for just one night. No strings. Just sex. But there were strings tying me up all over the place. Not the good kind of tied up either.

And then there was that hair of his.

I'd long ago made a pact with my college friends to never date a guy with better hair than me. Granted, I had an incredible head of hair and his wasn't better than mine, but it was better than most women's I knew. We'd all had terrible luck with long haired men. I don't know what it was, but it was a new level of arrogance every time I encountered one. Man-buns, in my world, either came with a man who wanted to live off the grid or thought he could create his own damn grid and you'd like it if he had anything to say about it.

So, there you had it. Long hair and my enemy. Choice made.

"Still a hard no, buddy." I sighed. My lips were still tingling from the soft kiss he'd placed on them.

He smiled and leaned his forehead to mine. "Ashlyn."

I closed my eyes and wished things were different for us. It looked like tonight wasn't my bits and bobs night. The only choice I would make would be whether to unpack Wanda the Wonder Wand or Virginia the Virginal Vibrator. One of them was going to have to perform their solo mission yet again. Or maybe this evening called for both of them to perform.

He leaned back and I immediately missed his heat and that damn fine body on mine. Tipping my head to the side, I studied his face, trying to figure out what was going through his mind. We both knew the score, so what was he playing at?

A hint of sadness floated by his face, but it was quickly gone.

"Rex, I—"

"Don't. I'm well aware of all of the reasons why us dating is a disastrous idea, Doctor Murphy."

"It's Doctor Murphy again, is it?"

"Easier this way. I've got to get going." He turned to go and I actually wobbled a little. I just needed him a tiny bit longer. Also, I was rip-roaring drunk and wearing three-inch stilettos.

"Wait." Oh Lord. The room spun and I regretted the shots I'd downed prior to coming out to the dance floor. Damn my sisters. Evil. Every last one of them. I briefly wondered where they'd all managed to skulk off to, but decided to take care of the more pressing concern first.

"Ashlyn." He grabbed a hold of me. "Hey? You okay?"

Nope. Definitely not okay. But he was going to be the last person I would ever tell. I plastered on a smile that rivalled any psycho clown smile you could think of. It felt crazy, so I could only imagine what it looked like.

He burst out laughing, so I didn't have to struggle to imagine all that hard. "I'm soooo good. Nothing to worry about. Just a little bit tipsy, that's all. And turned on. So turned on."

I slapped a hand over my mouth as my brain caught up. "Damn. Not turned on. Nope, not at all. Also, slightly nauseous. That probably cancels out the turned on."

He was staring at me, trying to figure out what in the hell I was playing at I'm sure. "Let's get you back to your friends." He grabbed my hips and tried to rotate me around while looking for my family.

"They're no friends of mine."

"No? You're not here with your friends?"

"No. They're my evil sisters and sisters-in-law. Pure, sadistic evil." Another wave of dizziness hit me just then and I grabbed a hold of his jacket to steady myself, leaning in really close to his beautiful face. "You have no idea what I'm wearing under this crazy dress. Want to know? Yes?" I slapped at his chest copping a not-so-secret feel. "Nothing. That's what I'm wearing. Not even any panties. I took them off in the bathroom because they were climbing inside my ass. God is going to strike me down well and good tonight, Rex. I'm going commando. Fucking commando! Evil, the lot of them."

"Ash! Are you going to introduce us to your friend?"

"Speaking of evil, here's the evil ringleader. Keeva, meet, um, Rex! Rex, that's it." I hiccupped and swayed a bit and felt his hand steady me at my back.

"Hey Tarzan. How'd ya know Ash?" Keeva, my sister without the filter, stared unabashedly up at Rex. As I followed her gaze and through my alcohol goggles, I saw she was kinda right. He did look a little like Tarzan. The OG Tarzan, not the Alexander Skaarsgard version. A little rough around the edges, but oh so very fine.

He threw his head back and laughed at Keeva, revealing two adorable dimples I suddenly felt like licking. Good Lord, what was wrong with me? This was why I didn't drink. Ashlyn Marie Murphy didn't lick the enemy. She gave the enemy the Murphy Mayhem. I giggled. I was thinking about myself in the third person and was now referring to the stupid name my brothers gave themselves when they banded together as kids and terrorized the neighborhood. It was official. I needed to get back home.

"I've used the good doctor's services recently. I own the farms that surround her."

I could see my eternal ally, my sister, tense up and prepare herself for one of her very favorite things. A verbal smackdown. It was all she had in her arsenal, tiny thing that she was.

"Ah, so you're the dickheaded asshole who's trying to buy up all her land."

"Yes, I suppose I am. Although, in my defense, my father is truly the bigger dickheaded asshole and the one who is the driving force behind the plans to purchase. If you want to differentiate between us, you add "big" to my dick. At least then, you know, you'd have a way to tell us apart when we're both being assholes."

"Jesus, I don't want to know about that and I'm not about to try to find out the truth of it," my sister barked out. "But the common theme here is *asshole*."

I needed to intervene before my little spitfire of a sister started a full-out brawl inside Galway's only dance bar.

"Okay, you two. Time to break it up. Keev," I turned to face her fully. "I'm tired and I'm feeling kind of nauseous. Can we go home now?"

I felt a hand at my back for a brief second and willed myself not to turn around. It didn't matter how badly I wanted to run my hands through that incredible mane of hair, or how much my fingers longed to trace the stubble ghosting his chin, I needed to clear my drunken head and remember who it was I was dealing with. This man was the enemy and if it's one thing the Murphys did good, it was remembering who the enemy was.

I mercilessly tamped down the craving in my core at his touch and moved away from him. "Come on, let's go guys. These shoes are killing me."

Keeva raised an eyebrow while still staring hard behind me, grabbed Sam, who appeared to be trying to twerk her way around the dance floor, and we went to go find Violet, who was likely still at the bar, sitting on a stool, wishing she was anywhere else.

Keeva grabbed my hand and pulled me behind her, not giving me time to hesitate. Glancing behind me, I met Rex's eyes and saw the heat flare, then get replaced with the coldness I had seen the other day. Well, if he was shutting down, so was I. I straightened my spine and gave it my all to walk out of there in a straight line, mostly failing miserably.

We grabbed Vi, hit the doors and spilled out into the cool Galway night. I braced for impact, expecting my sisters and sisters-in-law to jump in for all the gory details as soon as we got outside, but they were unexpectedly silent as we wound our way to Keeva's car.

We were all staying at the place she shared with her husband, Nixon, who was in turn, staying with my brother, Brennan, at his place. Bren and his wife Sam owned the family pub, Murphys, south of Galway in Brandon Bay, and it was typically our family's central gathering place. It was likely my brother Aiden was there as well, although he did have his daughter, August, to look after since Gray was back to being on Aiden lock-down now that they had another baby on the way. Since the first baby nearly killed her, and Aiden was an actual OB/GYN, our days of being able to see Gray outside were numbered.

But having kids in tow didn't stop us Murphys from heading out to the pub very often, so it was logical to assume Aiden was there with strict orders for Gray. As for Quinn, my hardheaded, often jerk of a brother, he was home with his twin babies and usually wouldn't be caught dead at the pub with the babies in tow. Quinn might have been born a Murphy, but his personality made me suspicious of the nature of his true origin on this earth. Something a little hotter and closer to Hell.

We found Keev's car and piled in, squeezing ourselves into the tiny Golf, sandwiched together while Keeva drove like a maniac through the winding streets of the city. No one said a thing. It was getting uncomfortable and I was definitely feeling nauseous.

"How can you all be falling asleep? This ride is so wild it's making me feel sick." I tried to adjust my rear end as I'd been relegated to the hump seat. Why the tallest person by miles was sitting in the middle was beyond me. "Did I miss something?"

Sam held up a hand, her unilaterally implied signal to save it. "Let's review, Ash. You've been a miserable bitch lately."

"I—"

"Nope, it's the truth and there's no sense trying to deny it. We're your family. We bear the brunt of it, so save it."

"Wow." There was nothing like being blindsided by someone you loved. The sobering process was in fast forward thanks to this car ride. "Okay, tell me how you really feel?"

"It's time for tough love, babe. Now, it's fine, 'cause we love you and all that, but sweetheart, something has to change. Between you and Quinn, it's...well, it's a lot of broody moodiness in this family."

"Hey!" Violet squeaked out from beside me. "Leave Quinn out of this. He's changed."

I turned to look at her with one eyebrow raised. "Seriously? He's still the same overbearing, egotistical asshole that he's been since the beginning of time. It's just that when you're around, he has multiple personality disorder."

"We were talking about your issues, Ash. Focus."

I turned back to face to the front and crossed my arms, completely uncomfortable with the scrutiny I knew was coming my way. How did we go from having the best time dancing and drinking to the third degree? Big Irish families were all sorts of things, but shy about their feelings, nope. If they were pissed at me for some reason, I was surprised it had taken them this long to come out with it, and that they had chosen this moment to unleash it.

"Fine. Tell me about all the shit you've been enduring. But I'm warning you, I'm just drunk enough to take it badly."

Violet leaned her head on my shoulders and sighed. She was the peacemaker. Whatever Sam was about to unleash on me was going to make her incredibly uncomfortable. She would be my ally in the rising tide.

Keeva was the angry spitfire. Sam was our leader and didn't take shit from anyone, man, woman or beast. Violet was my best friend and was equal parts shit-kicker to my butt and defender of my honor.

Sam turned around to face me and I could see she was struggling. "Out with it. Like ripping off a Band-Aid. Tell me what it is that's been bugging everyone so much, but tell me this first. Why didn't anyone tell me whatever it is I've done before we were cramped and drunk in Keeva's miniature car? I'm getting the most action I've gotten in years sitting on this hump, my buzz is coming down which is making me angry and I'm wearing heels for fuck sakes. Your timing leaves something to be desired."

Her eyes turned sympathetic and I knew tears weren't far behind, for all of us. This was how we rolled. We fought hard, but we loved hard too. That was the best part of being from a big family.

"Ash, we've all seen it. The past year, all you've been doing is working. Working, working, working. And over the past couple of months, you're snippy. Quick to bark at us when we're only trying to help."

"Help me with what? I'm perfectly fine."

"Are you? Really?"

"What's that supposed to mean? I'm here, aren't I?"

"Yes, but this is the first time any of us has seen you since Keev's wedding. Even Violet."

"Violet's been busy and I've seen her." I turned to face my best friend. "Right?"

"Yes," she said. "We've seen each other, but, well, not like this. Not like we used to."

"Well, I don't know why that responsibility falls only on me. You guys can come to me too, you know. I'm busy trying to run my business and save our family farm. I think I've kind of got my hands full here."

"You've taken that on alone, Ash." Violet spoke up beside me. "It doesn't have to be all on your shoulders."

I sighed. "It does, Vi. It does."

"Why?" Keeva finally joined into the fray.

"Because, guys, it's my name on the deed to that land. We all got something from mom and dad. Keev, you got money to start your business. Bren got the pub. Aiden got the manor house. And Quinn got...who the hell knows 'cause he's never said. I got the farm and the land to raise my horses on. Sam, I'd never expect Bren to come to any of us when the pub was struggling, even though of course we'd all do anything we could to help. It's just not how we roll."

My logic had hit true. I knew they meant well, but us Murphys were a stubborn lot. We operated in silos, be that good or bad. "Stupid, stubborn Murphy siblings," she muttered. "With your stupid martyr issues."

I smiled. "Sam, you live with the biggest, most stubborn of us all. He's our leader. You should know better than to ask me to share this burden. It's mine to figure out. And I will. I know I've cut myself off, a bit."

"More than a bit, Ash."

"You're right Vi. I'll try harder to drive you and Gray nuts, since you live next door and all."

"Okay, we'll have to settle for that promise, but you better start asking us to help out, or else. Now, on to the next issue."

"There's more?"

"Oh yes, but we'll need more alcohol for phase two. Keeva, peddle to the metal, please."

We rolled into the alley behind Keeva and Nixon's house, spilling out of the tiny car like a pack of high-class clowns. Laughing, I was thankful for my sisters, even if they drove me nuts. I supposed I had been fortunate their focus had been on everyone but me for a few years. We all had to take our turn on the Murphy Struggle Bus, and it looked like it was finally mine.

We stumbled into Keeva's incredible loft space, grabbing snacks and bottles of wine and whiskey for whatever phase two was going to require. I had a feeling I was in for a rougher ride but wasn't sure adding more alcohol was my best option or that I'd even get an option for that matter.

"Shot!" Sam shouted. We raised our glasses and clinked. We stared each other in the eyes to ward off bad luck and tossed back the Jameson. This was a very bad idea, but when it came to peer pressure, I was amongst the best and they knew I crumbled quickly.

"God! The burn!" Tears rolled down Violet's cheeks. "Ash! Shot!" She ruthlessly wiped away the tears. "If I'm going down, you're coming with me."

I rolled my eyes and threw back the shot like a pro.

"Out with it Ash. Your time is up. Who was the hottie from the club and why is he trying to destroy us?"

"He's not trying to destroy us." Whoa. Where did that come from? I didn't defend the McDaniels. I hated them. Clearly I wasn't focusing hard enough on defeating the enemy.

"Okay," Sam said. "Then what is he trying to do?"

"Well," I paused, considering my answer. I didn't want them to panic, because if they panicked, my brothers got involved. "His father's company is trying to buy my land to expand their holdings." I fiddled with my hands in my lap. Was it really that simple?

"What does that mean?" Sam was our businesswoman.

She might have left her superstar career behind, but she'd started up a production company that was becoming a huge powerhouse in the film industry. You didn't accomplish that with just connections. She was ruthless and powerful and freaking smart when it came to business. I really should have been looping her in on this whole shitshow. I was a vet. Bottom line, I took care of animals. I wasn't interested in the business side of things and lately that was showing.

Of course, I wanted my vet business to grow and prosper, but the rest was my business manager's job. I just healed animals. And rode my horses. Ever since this whole land thing had started I'd been drowning in stress. I truly didn't know what I was doing and was so damn tired of trying to figure it out.

A lone tear slipped out and I hiccupped. "Damn." Violet wrapped an arm around me and Gray leaned in. "Guys. I do need help. I don't *know* what it means. All I've been doing is getting angry, frustrated and stomping around work like everyone's the enemy. I don't want to lose my farm, but he's wearing me down. I'm just so damn tired."

"Shot!" Violet, grabbed the bottle and poured us all a round.

"Last one for me." Sam tossed it back and got up to go to the kitchen.

"Me to." I didn't want a hangover. I just wanted, well, I wasn't sure what I wanted. Outside of peace and quiet and possibly someone to share that peace and quiet with. Lately I was just going through the motions.

"The way I see it, you've got two options," Sam said as she came back with water for everyone. "You can sell the land to them, or you hire someone to grow the business side of the farm and just be a vet. You can't keep going full speed ahead without something giving. And the last thing we want, is for that something to be you. If you retreat any further into your life, you'll disappear. So, make a choice. What's it going to be?"

"I don't know, Sam," I whined and slammed my head down on the coffee table. "I'm not good at making decisions. Decisions suck."

"They don't suck. What sucks is your fear. What are you really afraid of?"

I looked anywhere but at them. "Disappointing mom and dad," I whispered. I wrapped my hands around my head and prayed for everyone to focus on someone else. Keeva was unusually quiet. I gathered my courage and looked her in the eye. "Keev?"

She raised a single eyebrow and gave me the patented Murphy stare. "Are you just about finished with your pathetic pity party?"

"No, as a matter of fact, I'm not."

"Get over yourself, Ashlyn. This isn't you. You're Ashlyn Murphy. Top of your class. Ball buster. Take no shit from anyone. My big sister. Feared by all. Not this wimpy, sad version of yourself. Make a choice. Don't blame mom and dad. They left you the land. They left me money. I've spent the money. It's not about the money, it's about us. Their kids. It's about our happiness and what that money could do for us. You've done what you wanted with it. It was never about the land, it was about the horses and your vet practice. So, make a decision. Sell or don't sell? But just make it."

I stared at her, knowing deep down she was right, but still not interested in admitting it. I needed to choose. Veterinary medicine or horse breeder. Being both was driving me into the ground. The other problem was, the last people I would ever want to bend to was the McDaniels. Well, bending to Rex McDaniel didn't seem all that bad. God, I was so messed up.

"I'm going to bed. Alone. Again." I got up and slowly

HOLLY MORTIMER

dragged my drunk and tired ass to the bed I was sharing with Vi.

"Oh please," my serious pain-in-the-ass sister yelled again. "And whose fault is that? Go be the martyr, sister dearest. You'll be alone for a freaking eternity with that attitude."

I slammed the door on her wishing, not for the first time, I was an only child.

CHAPTER SIX

REX

"*D*ad?" I heard for the thousandth time today. It was Sunday, the day we always devoted to each other. Miller was six and rarely ever stopped talking. I had a tendency to only half listen and it typically got me into a lot of trouble with her. I focused in on her instead of indulging in the replay of Ashlyn Murphy that had been going on inside my brain for the past twelve hours.

"Yup?"

"Is it always bad for dogs to eat chocolate?"

I stopped scrolling on my phone and looked at my daughter with a skeptical eye. Biased or not, Miller was kind of smart for her age and I felt like this was something she would already know, or at least know that Google often produced more accurate information than her dad. Alarm bells started going off inside my head and I mentally tried to remember the last time I'd seen that insane lab I'd gotten her to help with the transition of our move to Ireland.

"Why?" She started to turn away from me, but I could see the panicked look on her face. "Miller. Where's Elsa?"

To say Miller had an obsession with the movie Frozen

was a gross understatement. She had three options when getting dressed each morning. Elsa's gown, Anna's dress or her head to toe Frozen hoodie and leggings. Today, it was Elsa's gown.

"She's not feeling good, Daddy. She might have eaten some of your secret chocolate."

"Some? How did she get into my secret chocolate?" Shit, this was bad. On all fronts. So I loved chocolate. And yes, it was a secret, but that's only because everyone gave me the gears for it. Men were supposed to have obsessions with chips, beer, nachos, wings. I had a problem staying away from chocolate and since I'd moved to Ireland, it had only worsened. The chocolate here was next level.

Prior to becoming a parent, I stored my stash out in the open, but now that it was just me and Miller, I had to be the responsible one and pretend I didn't sneak chocolate at the end of every day. Apparently, all of my sneaking hadn't gone unnoticed and now I had my explanation as to why I could have sworn my stash was shrinking lately.

I ran into Miller's room and found Elsa lying on the floor, moaning and looking downright miserable. By the looks of her, she must have eaten the entire stash, not just a little bit. "Elsa, baby." I leaned down to stroke her head. "It's okay. We'll get you sorted, hang in there girl."

"Daddy," my daughter wailed and my kryptonite started sliding down her face. I simply could not handle her tears. She let them go so rarely that when they came, they undid me.

I scooped her into my arms and sat down in front of the dog. "It's going to be fine, Mills. Elsa's going to be just fine."

"But Daddy," she pulled in a sobbing deep breath. "She needs a doctor. Chocolate really does kill dogs. Oh Daddy!" She leapt off my lap and laid down beside Elsa.

I whipped out my phone and dialed the only person I knew in this godforsaken place who could help me.

"Hello?" Her deep, sexy voice came on the line and I shoved down all those stupid thoughts that I'd been trying so hard to unsuccessfully tamp down all day. "Who is this?"

"Ashlyn. It's Rex. I'm so sorry to bug you on a Sunday, but I really need your help and didn't know who else to call."

"Rex?" She took a minute and I could picture her sitting there, that glorious raven hair piled high on her head, her adorable black glasses perched on her nose, probably reading with a roaring fire, relaxing on a Sunday afternoon. "What's wrong?"

"It's my dog. She's eaten a significant amount of chocolate and it looks like she's not feeling so good."

"Give me your address. I'll need a few minutes to run to the barn to grab some supplies and in the meantime, keep an eye on her. She'll be fine for a bit. What kind of dog and how much does she weigh?" I could hear her rustling around and I involuntarily pictured her getting dressed. Parent of the year. Give me a dire situation and I'll think with my dick.

I let out a breath for the first time in the past ten minutes. "She's a lab. One year old, enormous. Around one hundred pounds"

"That's good. The bigger the better. I'm on my way."

I gave her the address and she hung up. I looked over at Miller and Elsa and took another deep breath. These two were my world. I'd become surprisingly attached to the little shithead of a dog since we'd gotten her. God knew my dad wasn't interested in anything more than the financial contribution I could make to his company. Nope, it was the three of us against the world. Ashlyn needed to hurry the hell up.

"Daddy, who was that?"

"That was my friend, Ashlyn. She's the vet I was telling

you about yesterday. She's coming over as quickly as she can."

She flung herself back into my arms and I laid us both down beside the dog, sandwiching her in between myself and Elsa, gathering the two of them into my arms.

"Oh, Daddy, is Elsa going to be okay? Is the vet coming fast enough?" Her little voice grabbed me by the heart and squeezed tight.

"Of course she is, Mills. Look at her. You know she's got a stomach made of steel, right? Remember that time she ate those rocks?"

She giggled and I relaxed a tiny bit, hoping like hell I was right. I didn't know what I would do to console her if the dog really didn't make it through.

We sat there like that for about twenty minutes and as I was debating whether or not to Google possible solutions to help the dog, the doorbell rang, saving me from paying a small fortune to the online VetChat.com service.

"That's her." I unwrapped my arm from around the two of them. "I'll be right back, Mills."

I jogged to the door, throwing it open against the driving rain that had been coming down all damn day. "Hey, thanks for coming over so quickly. Come on in."

She was carting the biggest bag I'd ever seen. It looked like she'd stuffed every possible option she'd need into it. "Can I get that for you?"

"I'm good. Where is she?" She brushed on by me. All business, which wasn't surprising based on how we left things last night.

Well, now was as good a time as any to let her know about Miller. There was no way to avoid it any longer. What she did with the information was going to be interesting. "She's in my daughter's room. Follow me."

I didn't stick around to see her reaction, just led the way

through our cottage to Miller's room, also known as the best shrine to Frozen on either side of the Atlantic. Most people had trouble believing I was a single dad who'd wanted sole custody of his daughter. I found the look on their faces generally amusing these days. I was used to their shock. Outside of our home, I would admit that "parent" wasn't my persona.

"Miller? This is my friend, Ashlyn. She's the vet I told you I called. Sweetheart, sit back and let her check out Elsa."

If she had questions, she didn't let on. Ashlyn plopped her bag down on the floor, sat down beside the dog and Miller and smiled. "So, Miller? What a crazy cool name." My daughter just stared at her, reverting back to her shy self I thought she'd left behind in the States. Unaffected, Ashlyn plowed ahead.

"What's your dog's name?"

"Elsa," Miller whispered.

"Oh, wow! Did you know I have a horse called Sven? Frozen is absolutely my favorite Disney movie!"

Miller's eyes lit up and the cold wall around my heart cracked just a tiny bit. Miller was my weakness and it ate me up that I had to move her here and that she only had me. She was an incredible child and I did my best, but she needed a woman in her life. The older she got, the more panicked I got when I thought about raising a girl on my own. But I wasn't interested in jumping the gun on that front. In fact, we mostly kept to ourselves out here in our little cottage.

I rarely dated and on the occasion I did, none of that ever touched Miller. I was very careful to make sure she had no idea what I got up to, or who I hung out with in the dating department. Not that I'd even entertained the thought of a relationship, since I'd done so spectacularly well with Miller's mom and all, but if it ever did happen, I would be incredibly picky as to the woman I integrated into our life.

"Okay Miller. Have you ever assisted a vet before?"

The ice sheared off a tiny bit more as I watched my daughter practically glow from the inside out. "No. Do you need an assistant?"

Ashlyn smiled and glanced up at me. Her smile faltered and I saw the uncertainty in her eyes. Raising one eyebrow I nodded for her to continue. No fucking way would I stop this now, even if having her here in my house was doing crazy things to my head. I'd only known this woman for a few days and she was doing a damn good job of turning my carefully constructed world upside down.

"I sure do. Okay, I need you to keep her calm and still. I'm going to give her belly a feel and listen to her insides. Then we'll have to get her up and outside so we can make her puke!"

"We—gross!" Miller wrinkled her nose and shifted so she could help Ashlyn better.

Ashlyn started to palpitate the dog's stomach, deftly moving her fingers around the beast's heaving stomach until she stopped and reached into her bag to pull out her stethoscope.

Hooking the device around Miller's neck, she fixed it into her ears. "Okay, ready to assist?"

Miller nodded her head, all business. "Yup. Ready."

She took the end of the stethoscope that enhanced the sound and placed it above the dog's heart.

"Am I close? Can you hear the heartbeat?"

Miller's eyes lit up and her smile was so wide, it practically encompassed her entire face. "Yes! I can hear it!"

"Excellent. Now, focus on the heartbeat and count out loud how many times you hear it beat. Can you do that? There's no shame in admitting that you can't count to one hundred. It's common, you know."

"I can totally count to one hundred. I'm not a baby!"

"Oh, my mistake." She turned and smiled up at me and I silently cursed and checked the lock around my heart. "Well, then, tell me when you're ready and we'll start counting. I'll time and you count and then we'll move on to the next thing. Ready?"

"Ready!"

"Go!"

Miller started counting and I leaned against the wall, basking in the parental glow of watching your child rise to the occasion. We'd moved here a few of months ago and Miller was not happy about it, but I'd needed to keep my job within the corporation and my dad needed someone to take over his evil empire in Ireland. Desperate times and all that. So here we were.

Truth be told, I hated shoving my humanity down every time I set foot inside my father's offices. The ruthless businessman had never been me, but it had been what I'd been groomed to be, and so it was expected of me regardless of how I felt about it. I felt the worst about it when I looked at my daughter and knew if she could see me while I worked, her opinion of me would be in the gutter. And now, watching Ashlyn treat her like her own, even after I'd been a colossal asshole to her, I knew I had a choice to make. My father expected me to take the company in the same direction as he had been when I took over and the easy thing to do would be to just let that happen.

But I was beginning to think it might be more fun to head in a new direction. One where the business model wasn't "grow at all costs" and be more in line with "grow with respect to the needs of the business and the community that supported it." I smiled to myself thinking about how my father would take the news of his company heading in a kinder, gentler direction. Maybe it would be better if I just made the changes and let him find out on his own. All of this was running through my head while Ashlyn worked on the dog.

The one thing I did know was that it was getting harder and harder to push Ashlyn to sell her land with every encounter we had. The more time I spent with her, the less interested I was in messing with her life.

"And...stop!" Ashlyn said. "Okay, so what did we get?"

"135. Is that good?"

"Well," Ashlyn said. "It's not ideal. I think to be on the safe side, we'll see if we can make Elsa here bring up her delicious chocolate treat. Are you up for the job?"

"Well, that depends." Miller sat back and took off the stethoscope.

"On what?"

"On how we do that. Do I have to shake her super hard? Turn her upside down?"

Ashlyn looked thoughtful. "Hm, well, even though those are tried and true methods that bring interesting results, we're going to use nature to do it for us. Well, nature and your dog's tendency to eat anything that comes near her."

"How?"

She rummaged around her bag and came up with some black pieces of rock inside a zippered bag. "With these magical things."

Miller's eyes grew and she looked adorably perplexed. "They're magic?"

"Not the kind you're thinking of. This, my friend, is charcoal. When dogs eat charcoal, it makes the contents of their stomach gurgle and churn and suck up all the goo inside their tummy that shouldn't be there. We'll also give her some medicine and eventually, the dog will barf everything up."

"Gross! Let's give it to her now."

"Agreed. Are you ready?"

"Well," Miller says. "What if she won't eat it?"

Ashlyn laughed. "I've never met a lab who wouldn't eat anything that they came in contact with. Have you?"

"Well, I don't know many labs, but I know Elsa and she will eat ANYTHING!"

"Exactly. I also brought my secret weapon. Peanut butter. So, ready?" She pulled out the charcoal and peanut butter and a spoon and gave it Elsa, who just as predicted, lapped it up and sniffed around for more. Then she put some medicine into another spoonful of peanut butter and the dog lapped it up too.

"She's not puking?" Miller crouched down and listened to the dog's stomach.

"It takes a couple of minutes, but let's get ready. Since it's raining out, I brought my special puke towels so Elsa can do it inside and not get it everywhere. Can you help me spread them out around her? They'll absorb the vomit."

They got to work and just as they finished Elsa hopped up and proceeded to puke all over the puppy pads Ashlyn had spread out. She rubbed the poor dog's back, muttering soothing messages to her as she ejected all the garbage in her stomach.

"Gross, Elsa. Oh look," Miller yelled. "Her food's still in there!"

"Yup. Labs are gulpers. They just hoover up their food so fast it takes a long time to digest. So, if I had to guess, she ate all that chocolate just before or right after she ate her regular food."

Miller looked up at me and smiled. "Dad! Look, Elsa's gonna be okay. Doctor Ashlyn saved her!" God, this kid. She undid me every time she looked my way.

I flopped down on the floor trying to avoid the puke and looked right into Ashlyn's eyes. It didn't matter what we were supposed to be. I wasn't Rexford McDaniel the Third, the man who was trying to take her land, and she wasn't

Ashlyn Murphy, the woman who was stubbornly refusing to give in to our requests. We were Ash and Rex. United in our mission to save Princess Elsa, the lab who ate too much chocolate.

I mouthed a silent "Thank you" to her over Miller's head and looked down into the damn dog's eyes. "Princess Elsa. I don't ever want to see you eating anything other than your dog food ever again. Got it?"

She just stared at me and I knew I'd be here again real soon. And funny enough, I was totally looking forward to it.

CHAPTER SEVEN

ASHLYN

started rolling up the extra absorbent pads I kept in my medical kit wanting desperately to get out of Rex's house before the feelings I was having intensified. His call had caught me off guard until I fell back on my old faithful, emergent care training. I was good in a crisis. I wasn't going to exactly call this a crisis, but to his adorable daughter, Miller, it was one of epic proportions.

Miller. Jeez, he had a child. A daughter. I had been discreetly looking around, trying to determine if there was a wife I hadn't expected either. So far, I couldn't quite firmly decide one way or the other.

"Mills," he said. "Why don't you take Elsa outside and let her get some fresh air?"

"Good idea. Miller, I'm going to warn you. She's probably going to blow up from the other end too. Be prepared for a poop-plosion. It's not gonna be pretty for Elsa for the next twelve hours. It looks like the rain has died down so she shouldn't get too wet."

Miller jumped up and the dog followed her as if nothing

had just happened. That was the thing about labs. They were the best rebounders I'd ever nursed back to health.

Rex knelt down beside me with a garbage bag and I involuntarily shifted over a little. God, this man. He made me so uncomfortable.

"I don't bite."

Of course he noticed. There didn't seem to be much this man missed. "I never said you did."

Keep busy, Ash.

I just needed to keep my head down, and my eyes averted to that incredibly toned forearm. What I wasn't expecting was the scent. You'd think that around all the dog puke and medicines that his damn intoxicating smell wouldn't stand a chance. But there it was. The one thing I couldn't shut off.

"Are you okay?" he asked.

"Yes." My high pitched squeal was pathetic. I was pathetic. The girls would be so disappointed in me, again. "I'm fine. Just trying to get cleaned up so you two can get back to your night. Elsa should be just fine, but—"

He grabbed my wrist and put a stop to my frantic bag-packing activities. I was forced to look him in the eye and was alarmed by their colour. I'd never been this close to him in lighting that was meant for illuminating a space and not for masking patron's flaws. "Can I help you?" I threw as much indignation as I could muster into my voice.

"Thank you."

"You're welcome?"

"I know you don't like me and I know helping me is probably the last thing you want to do, but seriously, thank you."

"It's my job. Saving animals. It's what I do. No big deal, really."

We both looked down at his hand on my wrist and he immediately dropped it. Damn it all. I wanted his hand back on me. What a disaster I was. The first man I'd been interested in in forever and it was the one guy I could never have. Classic Ashlyn Murphy romance. I really knew how to pick 'em.

I cleared my throat and finished cleaning up. He held out his hand to help me up and I suddenly became paralyzed.

"It's just a hand, Ashlyn."

God, the way he said my name. Shit. This was bad. Weepy, romantic Ashlyn was supposed to be firmly in the past. This version of me wasn't who I had become. I needed to go before I was pulling out his ridiculous man-bun and running my hands through that glorious mane of hair. Dammit, I was giving up romance novels for good this time. Not just for Lent.

I ignored his offered hand and got up on my own, firmly letting him know I was all business. Doctor Ashlyn Murphy. I needed that distinction now more than ever. I wasn't here because we were friends. He was the exact opposite. The enemy. He was trying to take away everything I'd worked so hard to hold on to. It wouldn't do me any good to forget that.

"Okay, well, I'll have my office send over the invoice. Please tell Miller it was great meeting her and let me know if Elsa's disposition doesn't improve over the next twelve hours. But, I think she's going to be fine."

I turned to go and once again, found myself trapped by his hand. "Ashlyn." *Dig deep Ash*, I whispered to myself. Enemy.

"Yes?" I turned my head to find him looking incredibly conflicted and hot. Yes, there was no denying it. This man standing here was incredibly hot.

"We're just about to have dinner. There's enough for ten people. Want to stay?"

Oh dear God. It just keeps getting worse. He cooks. Dinner for his family. That reminded me. "What about your wife? She'd probably find having dinner with the vet a little weird."

He smiled and I knew. I just knew I'd pissed off someone who had influence with the Big Guy up there. Perfect, straight teeth. Crinkly eyes and a freaking dimple. Make that double dimples. Life wasn't fair. This was just too damn hard. "No wife. Miller's mom and I haven't been together since she was born. I raised Millsy on my own since her mom walked out and left her without looking back when she was two months old."

I might as well just strip naked and give the devil his due. Let's review. Single dad since the birth of his daughter. Owned a lab. Hot as sin. Hair that shouldn't be seen on a man's head, but nonetheless, there you had it. I assumed he must love horses as much as I did. Life didn't fight fair. The human standing here in front of me couldn't be real! Enemy, I reminded myself. He was the enemy. Except the word didn't have the same effect it once had.

"I don't—"

"Dad!" Miller chose that time to race in from the yard. "She's perfect. Elsa's totally all better. See?" She came over and dragged her dad over to the garden doors. "Look at her. She's chasing squirrels like a crazy dog just like she usually does."

She turned to me and I saw the mini female version of her father staring directly at me. Long, gently curling dirty-blonde hair. Strong nose and jaw. Two tiny dimples on either side of her wide smile. "Thank you Doctor Murphy. Thank you so much for saving Elsa. I don't know what I'd ever do without her. She's the only thing I love about Ireland. Well, her and my dad. But that's definitely it. Everything else about being here is awful."

"You're very welcome, Miller. It makes me so very sad to

hear you don't love Ireland. What is it about Ireland that you don't like?"

"It's boring. Dad is always working and everyone at school hates me because I'm different and talk like an American. And, Grandpa is so mean. Like, the meanest meanie ever. And I know, Dad always says he's family and we just have to listen from one ear and let it go out the other ear, but man, he is so mean. And he's always bossing dad around. And he might say he likes horses, but he really doesn't. I can tell these things."

"Well, that's a lot of reasons that I can totally get behind. It's no wonder you hate Ireland." I smiled at the adorable girl. "Maybe one day I'll get the chance to change your mind."

"Can you stay for longer?" She looked at me with those big eyes and I was hit with a sense of longing I wasn't ready to dive into. "Please don't say no. We never have anyone over here. Come on. We could play a game!" She had grabbed both my hands and I didn't know what to do.

I looked at Rex and his eyebrows had moved up his forehead and his mouth was hanging open. "Ah, yes? Sure. Yes, you should stay. We make a mean bowl of popcorn and as I've already told you, dinner's nearly ready. But of course, as Miller said, we're recluses here and things might get awkward."

Get awkward? We were way beyond that. "Ah, sure. I can stay. But just for an hour."

"Yes! I'll get Monopoly. Dad never lets me play it because he says it's a game for when we have more than just me and him." She swept on by and disappeared into her bedroom, only to pop back out a few seconds later with the game.

"I'm sorry, Ashlyn—"

"It's fine," I said over top of him. "Let's just play, okay?"

Rex went to take their dinner out of the oven and Miller and I moved to the coffee table in their tiny living room that

Miller had cleared and was now deeply involved in setting up the game. There was something so endearing about this little family I had wanted so much to detest. After last night, I didn't want to feel anything else for this man, but the universe just kept testing me and throwing me curve balls where he was concerned. Every time I thought I had him figured out, bam. Curve ball right to the head.

Today it was finding out the demon's spawn was a single dad of the most adorable six year old and a lab. My Achilles heel. Labs and kids. I flopped down on the floor across from Rex and Miller and proceeded to lose myself in a rousing game of Monopoly and dig in to the best Irish stew I never thought I needed.

* * *

AN HOUR later I found myself running around the house, hands in the air, screaming with joy at having passed Go and collected the win! "Yes! Yes! Take that Mr. Shoe. The thimble just kicked your butt!"

It was official. I'd lost my mind and trouncing on a six-year-old was stepping way across the line. I admit, I was drunk on the power of my Monopoly win and was acting like a lunatic. But for some reason, I was struggling to care. I was used to playing with my own siblings and their kids and in our family, there were zero boundaries.

"Doctor Murphy," Miller yelled. "You're going crazy. And didn't anyone ever teach you that it isn't nice to make people feel bad about losing a game?"

"Miss Miller, I am feeling a little crazy tonight." I smiled at her and she stuck out her tongue at me, turned on her heel and marched into her room, slamming the door behind her.

At this point I started spinning with my arms out and realized that I'd officially lost my marbles and become a horrible person at the same time. A strong pair of arms encircled me from behind, stopping my celebrations and brought me crashing down to earth with a force I hadn't seen coming. "You really are a sore winner, you know?"

I closed my eyes and leaned back just a little. Just enough to get a sense of that large, hard chest supporting me from behind. I took a deep breath, grabbed his hands, leapt out of his hold and spun around to face him.

"I know. This girl right here," I pointed at myself. "And you can go ahead and call me a horrible person, because you'd be right. But only when it comes to games. I'm also a sore winner. And if you'd played a board game with me before, you'd have known that before we started. My nieces and nephew and all my siblings know better than to ever offer a seat at the game table to me. I drop my dignity at the door. What are you gonna do about it, Rexford McDaniel the Third?"

Silence fell between us and the next thing I knew, his lips were on mine and my mouth was being punished for my bad behavior. He grabbed my face in his hands to hold me still and God help me, my hands moved to grab frantically at his shirt, scrambling, searching for something to hold on to. He suddenly pulled back and let go, looking as shocked as I felt.

"Daddy?" Miller called from behind her door. His forehead came to rest on mine and I was incredibly thankful for his daughter. What were we thinking? Stupid Monopoly, making me lose my mind.

"Yes, Mills?" he called back, still looking like he was trying to sort out a lot of what had just happened in his own head.

She opened her door and came out. "Are you done celebrating, Doctor Murphy?"

"Yup. I'm so sorry I made you feel bad, Miller." I walked over to her and held out my arms. "Hug it out?"

She flew in and grabbed me around the legs, resting her head on my stomach.

"Okay," I said releasing her. "I've got to run."

I gathered up my medical bag, studiously avoiding looking at her dad. "Could we have a rematch one day?" she asked.

I looked at Rex who appeared to be looking at anything but me. "Mills, she's not—"

"Of course. One day."

We locked eyes and I tilted my head in a non-verbal challenge. Whatever it was we had just shared, it had shaken things up inside me. He was still the enemy. But now I wasn't sure if everything I'd thought I knew about the enemy was accurate. The one thing I did know was that I needed some space to figure him out.

"Bye guys." I turned and left, chewing on my bottom lip, trying to sort out who in the hell Rexford McDaniel really was, and why I was alternating between feelings of anger, frustration and undeniable lust.

CHAPTER EIGHT

ASHLYN

J walked into the barn the next day agitated and looking for a fight. Tossing and turning all night, I'd gotten a rotten sleep and was now in the foulest of foul moods. All I could think about was that man and his damn dog. Not to mention my kryptonite. A child. When you added it all up, man plus dog plus child, it was the holy trinity of things that brought Ashlyn Murphy to her knees. And the last place on earth I wanted anyone to find me was down on my knees.

Well, in the metaphorical sense that is. On rare occasions I'd been known to explore the floorboards with a mission in mind.

"Argh," I screamed. "Enough."

"Okay, I wasn't aware I was pushing any boundaries, yet?" Ox said while pressed up against a wall, seeming to be trying to make himself as thin as he could possibly be.

"I wasn't talking to you."

"Well, and for that, I'm incredibly grateful." He moved around me muttering to himself about something that better not have been *time of the month* or he'd get an earful from me that he'd never gotten before.

It was true. My miserable mood was probably going to ruin the day for everyone who got anywhere near me. I had no idea how Rex had gotten to me this way. The man was so incredibly annoying with his ability to affect me, for good or bad. I needed to focus on the job I had to do. I had a busy day in the clinic and then had unfortunately agreed to dinner at my brother's house.

I made a quick pit stop in my office to grab a hair tie and stopped short at the entryway. "What in the hell are you doing in here?"

Lounging in my favourite thinking chair in the corner of my expansive office was the man who had me so vexed. In all his freaking glory. Stretched out, every inch of his incredible body was relaxed, as if all the feelings I'd been dealing with all night long were not even a passing bother to him. What a fucking dick.

"Princess. We've got unfinished business."

"Princess? I find that name offensive and I'd like it if you didn't use it."

He raised a single eyebrow and smiled and my insides did a little flip. Traitorous insides. Stupid, stupid Ashlyn. I needed to focus. I had a busy day and dinner with family. Shaking him off immediately was absolutely necessary in order to salvage the morning.

"Did you need something? I'm in a hurry. I've got a clinic to conduct, patients waiting."

He hesitated. What was he up to? "I need a favour."

Now it was my turn to raise my eyebrows. Both of them. To the sky. "Interesting. I'm not in the business of granting favours to people who're trying to take away everything I've worked for. That seems to be more your family's thing. You know, I'll do you a favour and then you'll owe me kind of thing."

Chewing his bottom lip, he silently took stock of whatever it was he was here for. I reminded myself whatever it was, it wasn't my problem. I repeated that over and over to myself. If I was ever going to save my farm, I had to start standing up to the man reclining in my favourite chair, who apparently needed something from me. I couldn't trust him and it was high time I started remembering that. Great kisser or not. And now that kiss was back on replay. Damn him and his full, kissable lips of torture.

He fluidly rose from the chair, almost as if he defied the laws of gravity and I braced myself against my desk. He was good at this game. He'd been playing it way longer than I had. Lots of practice to be had on his game. My game? I didn't have any such thing. Nada game.

He was wearing a freaking suit, already, at 8:30 in the morning. A navy suit, with one of those crisp, white, tailored shirts underneath the jacket. My eyes weren't messaging my brain right now, they were just frozen. My circuits were broken, again. Like an Instagram Boomerang, bouncing up and down Rex's body, repeating the pattern over and over until the only thing you could do was tap to move on.

My brain? It wasn't moving on. It was thinking about boys. One single boy, actually. That's it. Even after the disaster that was last night. Even though it was Monday morning, my least favorite day of the week. Even though the man stalking towards me was my sworn enemy, my brain was stuck on, "boys good." Four years of vet school and my brain had dialed back the clock to fifteen-year-old Ashlyn.

I made the fatal error of calming myself with a deep breath in. The man had even taken the time to put on cologne. Who did that on a Monday morning? Mondays were for barely surviving the morning and living for lunch. That's it.

To divert the impending doom, I ordered my eyes downward and zoomed in on my old, beat-up Blundstones. My standby footwear when I was working in my clinic. Sneakers got awfully slippery when they came up against a pile of horse shit or doggy pee.

Blunnies, my favourite comfy jeans and a T-shirt versus fancy-pants with his hair wild and loose. Samantha would have been so disappointed in me.

He came to a stop directly in front of me, almost toe to toe. He stood there, not moving while I desperately tried to plan my escape. Granted, escaping from my own office was odd, yes, but still, I needed out. He slowly raised one of his hands, using one long, glorious finger to gently tilt my chin up until my eyes had only one choice. Looking at him, I knew the fight to control my libido was going to be considerably harder than I had anticipated.

"Ashlyn."

"Yes?" My breathing had become erratic, I was sure my pupils were dilated and I had a death grip on the edge of the desk behind me.

"I'm sorry."

"Sorry?"

"Yes, sorry. For my behavior last night." He was still holding my eyes in his gaze so I took the time to search. What was he up to? His eyes gave no clues and I tried to shake my head free of his hold.

"No need to apologize. For a kiss? Pshaw, please. It was nothing. I forgot who you were for a moment. I shouldn't have and for that, I'm sorry too. You didn't need to come here to say you're sorry. What is it you really want? What favour? Huh?" And I was afflicted again with nervous verbal diarrhea.

"Princess, don't."

"I asked you not to call me that and I'd appreciate it if you listened to my wishes for a change."

He smiled and even his damn teeth were hot. I was struggling not to release one hand and gently run it over the perfect scruff of his chin, where I knew I'd feel a roughness softened by the fine hairs in between. I stopped myself before I got too carried away and started imagining how the scruff would feel between my legs.

He closed his eyes and let out a long breath and I took that moment of release from his tractor beam eyeballs to compose myself. I had patients to see, a farm to save and a very large glass of red wine waiting for me at the end of what was sure to be an incredibly long day.

He opened his eyes, used his free hand to tuck an errant piece of hair behind my ear and it was my turn to close my eyes. The image of me kissing him last night came charging in and I knew whatever I'd done wrong in my life, I might have still earned myself a guardian angel. One who was on duty to remind me of all the reasons why he needed to go.

"Listen—" That scruff brushed up against my cheek and the butterflies took flight. I could feel his warm breath against my ear, my most sensitive zone. Oh, he was good. If I had a guardian angel, Rex most certainly was being guided by his own personal devil.

"I said I was sorry," he whispered. "That was my favour. Your time. To hear my apology. That's all."

"I—"

He pulled back, put his hands in his pockets, shuttered his eyes, took off, leaving me leaning against my desk, unsure of what had just happened, but feeling like I'd just made it through some sort of natural disaster. I needed a moment to compose myself before I went searching around a horse's genitals and life became mundane once again.

I laughed to myself. Only an equine vet would think checking on a horse who was about to birth her first baby with my hand up her lady bits was mundane.

"Something funny?" Ox had taken Rex's place and was now standing in front of me, looking at me like I'd lost my damn mind.

"No! Actually, not at all. Nothing is funny at all!" I practically yelled at him.

He held up his hands in the long-standing sign of surrender. "Okay, Ashlyn. It's just that, well…" He had the decency to look uncomfortable. I knew where this was going. "Well, *he* was just here. And I thought the last thing he would ever bring to the table is a sense of humour."

"Oh, he's got one, my friend. It's just a sick and twisted version of what most people think passes for humour." I slipped on my lab coat over my T-shirt and ushered him out of my office. The office that I had designed to provide sanctuary. Peace. Serenity. The very same office that now held the scent of a man who could very easily tear me and my family apart with his "sense of humour." A man who I needed to avoid at all costs from this point forward.

CHAPTER NINE

REX

*J*didn't know what the hell I was doing, but I knew I was walking a dangerous line. An all-too-familiar line. I was pretty sure I shouldn't be getting anywhere near Ashlyn Murphy if we were both going to come out of this unscathed.

I pulled into our offices and shoved the car in park. I needed a breather before I went inside and had to face the giant asshole, also known as my father. He'd be expecting a report on how the negotiations were progressing and it pained me to think about having to tell him that the negotiations weren't actually progressing at all. That I was too enamored with the one person who I needed to negotiate with in order to take her land from her at the lowest amount of money possible. I needed to stop showing up like I'd just done at her offices. And I sure as shit had to stop calling her to come rescue me or my dog at my house.

I got out and walked into the stark glass building that seemed to have landed in the middle of the Irish countryside from outer space, it was so obviously not of this earth. Of course, my father would have had to build it just like this. A giant fuck-you to the people and the land he cared so little for.

His claim that Ireland owed him a blood debt of some sort was insane but he'd never give it up. Some sort of family history from the dark ages I was sure, but to his face, I'd never admit he was fighting a fight he'd never win. This country did something to you, even when you weren't here looking for it. For me, it was something amazing. For him, it was always the opposite.

Since Miller and I had come here, I'd found a sense of peace that I wasn't sure was ever in the cards for us. Her mother being prone to hysterical dramatic parenting and having done a number on our daughter's head, I knew coming here was our last chance. As long as he was alive, my father had me on a short leash. He controlled my money until the day we would decide that in his eyes, I could handle it without squandering it. It was enough money for me to continue to put up with his bullshit. I didn't do it for myself. I did it for Miller. She'd never see a dime until I could make him believe we'd live up to his insane standards.

"Good morning, Mr. McDaniel. Shall I get your usual coffee then?"

"Good morning, Maisie. That'd be perfect."

Maisie Ronan was the only good thing about working in this corporation. She was the granny I never had and I looked forward to seeing her every day I had to spend in the office. She had taught me in a few short months how parenting should really be. She both mothered and smothered me and since I'd grown up with a "children are to be seen and not heard" set of parents, I fully tolerated it all. I wanted Miller to know this kind of mother existed.

I settled in behind the behemoth desk my father insisted I have as Maisie came back in with my morning ritual.

"Here's your coffee and this morning I've got you your favourite, chocolate chip."

I smiled up at her falling just a little further in love with her. "Maisie, this is exactly what I needed today. I have a feeling—"

"You have a feeling about what, boy?"

Fuck. That happiness bubble didn't last very long. I should have known the old dick would pounce this early on a Monday. Maisie gave me the googly eyes and scooted away, leaving me alone with my father. She'd pay for that one later.

"Nothing. What's up?"

Not bothering to come in and sit like a normal parent, he strode to stand his Lordshipness over me while I sat and tried desperately to ignore my cookies. God, I felt like I was five and had been caught with forbidden food in my mouth again.

"What's happening with the Murphy land? I hope you're not dillydallying. I need to secure that land to move forward."

"The Murphys are proving to be harder to negotiate with than we initially had anticipated."

I could see the never-ending disappointment in his eyes. Didn't matter much anymore. I was immune to it after all this time. What I wasn't immune to was the inevitable threats that came after that look.

"Do I need to remind you of your request to me? We had a deal, son. Your end of the bargain needs to be complete before I can ensure my end. If you want your daughter to remain in your hands, and not in that sorry excuse for a mother you chose, you're going to have to close the deal. I don't need to remind you that you're running out of time. Your vacation here is quickly coming to an end."

I hated him. I hated that he had me by the fucking balls and he knew it. Miller's mother might have been a self-absorbed bitch who didn't care a fuck about her daughter, but she was well aware of what a tremendous bargaining tool Miller was. She wanted the money that went along with Miller's last name and wasn't going to stop at anything to get it. I was looking with hatred at the one person on earth who could ensure Miller stayed with me, here in Ireland, where she belonged.

I hadn't always been the best father figure and my ex had made sure my father was aware, you know, should he ever need to control me. He had the power to ensure my ex-wife stayed off of the custody agreement. He also had the power to keep me legally in Ireland. I was well and royally fucked.

"Understood, father."

He smiled, if you could call it that. It looked like more of a grimace to me. "Excellent. I expect to have those documents on my desk by the end of the week, then."

"Fine."

He wrapped his knuckles on my desk twice, his signature exit sign, and walked out of my office having no idea how much I wanted to throw something heavy and lethal at his head. I spun my chair around to stare at the rolling green countryside and wondered how I'd made so many damn mistakes when it came to my heart.

My therapist would have a heyday with this new progression. I'd gone and gotten involved, yet again, with a woman who had the power to destroy me. It seemed I had mommy issues after all.

"Now, stop that, Mr. McDaniel. You've nothing to worry about. You're going to use that charming personality of yours and convince Doctor Murphy to part with her farm and you and Miller can stay here with us, happy as clams." She busied herself with tidying my office while I talked myself down off the ledge I was balancing precariously on.

"Oh Maisie, that's just it. This particular woman appears to be completely immune to my charms. In fact, I think the more charming I try to be with her, the more she dislikes me." I spun back around and plunked my head down on my desk, wrapping my hands around my neck and took a deep breath.

Think, idiot. There had to be a way to convince Ashlyn that selling her farm to my father was in her best interests. I supposed the first thing I had to convince her to do was to talk to me again. After last night's disaster and this morning's creeper routine, I was going to have to pull out all the stops and somehow keep my soul intact. I had a feeling I was going skirt that fucking line again and what had started out as a mission that needed to be completed at all costs, I suddenly wasn't sure I was willing to pay the price.

There had to be something I could use to get her to sell without compromising my promise to Miller that I would always be a good person. Six-year-olds see more than we give them credit for. Since we'd come to Ireland, she'd been watching me sink further and further into my father's ways. She'd watched me on more than one occasion say and do things I swore as a child growing up I'd never do.

The one thing she didn't know was that as her dad, I'd pretty much do anything for her. Anything to keep her with me for as long she'd have me. Keep her out of the money hungry, greedy hands of her mother, who only cared about the dollars that came with Miller. Every once in a while she'd rear her head looking for more money to support what vie for power she was on at that time. She'd threaten me with all the things she claimed to know and make sure my father was aware of her threats. Then he would pay up and we'd be back to the beginning. She was exhausting.

I felt sick about it, but it was time to up my game with Ashlyn. I needed to find her weakness and I was pretty sure I knew just how to do it.

Without giving myself any time to rethink my plan and

for my morals to come raging up to the surface to stop me, I grabbed my suit jacket, shoved Maisie's remaining cookie in my mouth and flew out of the office.

"I'm heading to the barns, Maise, and I'm not sure when I'll be back." I didn't stop to look at her. I knew the disappointed look on her face would be the one thing to stop me in my stupid tracks.

CHAPTER TEN

ASHLYN

*T*uesday. The day after Monday. That was about all I could really say about Tuesday. I looked up at the clock and could hardly believe it was only ten. My stomach was growling. The morning had been chaotic at best, insanity at the worst, and in the back of my mind were the events of the past forty-eight hours. I'd ruthlessly shoved those thoughts aside, but now, as I sat down at my desk in my office to try to find a snack, Rex's early morning visit yesterday was on replay in my mind.

After Sunday night's kiss and run, I never thought he'd have the balls to show up for more. And to apologize at that. I was beginning to learn there were more sides to Rexford McDaniel III. Father, son, business man and well, pure male. The problem was, I kept forgetting he was the bad guy He could be charming and goofy all he wanted, but that wasn't going to change the fact he wanted my land. For what, I had no idea, but it probably wasn't to preserve it.

I flopped down on my favorite chair and pictured him lounging there too. Damn. Was there nowhere I could go to get away from the vision of that man?

My phone chimed an incoming text and I groaned, looking up to where I imagined The Big Guy ran the show. "Really? You think this is funny?"

I looked at the text from Rex and wondered what kind of cruel joke fate was playing on me.

Hey. Again, I'm sorry for how I behaved last night.

…

I saw those three mysterious dots travelling across my screen signaling more was coming from him.

I have a problem.

I was weak. My self-imposed moratorium on contact with him looked like it was already coming to an end. Lasted a whole four fucking hours. I was a colossal disappointment to all females.

Yes?

Remember how my vet was out of the country last week and I had that injured horse?

Yes?

Well, I've got another urgent injury I need looked at. Any chance you could pretend you like me just a tiny bit, set aside your hatred and come here? Come on. Do it for Hazel!

Who's Hazel?

The pregnant horse who needs to give birth. Imminently.

I sighed and gave him back the three mystery dots. He didn't play fair. Fuck me sideways on Sunday, of course I was going to give in to him. Again. Just for shits and giggles, I gave him the three dots, then backspaced so they disappeared. Then started typing again just to mess with him.

It'll cost you. I'm swamped today.

Of course. I'll pay you your fee and then some. You're entirely worth it. In fact, I should just hire you! Except, you're much too busy with your own clinic, and your own farm and whatever else it is you've got going on.

…

I countered with the dots while I gave my head a shake. He knew I couldn't resist a complicated birth. Somehow he'd uncovered my biggest weakness, complicated births. Stupid Laney and her stupid defection. I absolutely loved helping a horse deliver safely. There was nothing like the rush afterwards. Like you'd been given a front row seat on an ancient mystery being revealed.

I decided to keep him guessing as I grabbed my keys and left my office for the first building in the outbuildings that were a part of my property. I had four in total. Two beautiful barns. One containing my vet practice and one holding my horses. The converted barn I just left was my private office space and the building I was headed for, my reception area and small animal clinic. I was proud of what I'd built. When our parents had passed away, they had left me and my siblings a piece of the country that had raised our mother. Being that we were all somehow ingrained with the entrepreneurial spirit, mostly all of us had used it to begin our lives here in Ireland and dabbled in starting businesses. With the exception of the black sheep, Quinn, of course.

I slipped into the back door and immediately knew getting out of here unseen wasn't going to be something I could accomplish today.

"And then I told him, I'm not interested, Quinn. Socializing is how normal people grow and survive. Living in isolation is soul-crushing. The babies need friends. And none of the moms in the mommy group are going to try to hurt them. No one's stealing our babies. Most people are good, decent humans."

I could see Violet talking to Sarah, my administrator slash everything else around here person. She was talking about my stubborn, obnoxious, reclusive brother, Quinn. They had twins six months ago and Quinn was reacting just as we all had predicted he would. Like an arrogant overbearing asshole.

They lived three doors down from me, on the other side of my brother and his girlfriend Gray, who only lived on our land part-time. The rest of the time, they lived in Dublin where my brother, Aiden was a doctor and Gray was a librarian. It was yet another reason I couldn't give up the farmland behind our houses. We all shared this land, even if the deed was in my name. It was a part of who we were.

"Would you just give that moron a smack on the side of his head and be done with it? Why give him the option of dictating where you take the babies?" I came up behind Vi and engulfed her tiny body in a bear hug. I rarely got to see her anymore, what with her twins, my caveman brother and her bakery business. She was incredibly busy. "Whatcha doing here Vi?"

"Escaping your overbearing, asshat of a brother."

"Mmmm, yup, that sounds about right. Want to go for a ride?"

"Yes!" Her smile was instant and a pang of sadness hit me. I hadn't been the best friend to Vi over the past few months. I'd been so wrapped up in all the land drama, that I'd closed myself off to my family.

"Aren't you supposed to be working right now?" I asked her. Violet owned the local bakery and catering business and was rarely sighted anywhere but there or at home with her twins.

"I'm taking some time off." Her eyes were looking anywhere but in my direction.

"Violet. Why are you taking time off?"

"Because Quinn decreed it." She looked me square in the face and raised both eyebrows.

I rolled my eyes and grabbed my keys from the desk. "Of course he did. I should have known better than ask. Come on, Red. You can help me help a mare give birth. And you'll be a fabulous buffer."

We exited my office space and walked over to my Range Rover. "Buffer?" she said. "What does that even mean?"

We got in and I started the engine, turning to check I had my supplies in the back like I normally did. I saw Ox standing in the field, his hands on his hips, staring at me. I waved and turned back around, putting the vehicle in drive.

"What's his deal, anyway?" Violet asked.

"Who? Ox? He doesn't have a deal, I don't think?"

"Oh," she laughed. "He sure does. Are you blind?"

I turned to fully look at her before turning out of my drive and onto the road. "Are you crazy? It's Ox! He's only concerned with Ox. And he definitely isn't interested in me. I'm just his boss."

She laughed out loud and raised one eyebrow, giving me the classic hairy eye. Looking beyond her as we passed Aiden's house, I could see Quinn standing outside their house, holding one of the babies, with his other hand on his hip. His patented glare reaching us even at this distance. Violet looked over just in time to see him grab his phone from his pocket. Her phone started to ring inside her handbag and I burst out laughing as she waved to her boyfriend, smiling like a lunatic while digging through her purse to answer his call.

"Quinn," she said.

"Where in the hell are you going?" He was so irate I could hear him through the phone even though he wasn't on speaker.

"Ash needed help and I happened to have been available. Remember? Remember when you told me I needed to take time off work? That I was addicted to working?"

He must have lowered his voice because I couldn't make out what he was saying from that point forward. I gave them as much privacy as an enclosed space could, and paid attention to the winding Irish roads. My mind drifted back to what Vi had said about Ox.

There was zero chance he was interested in me. He'd have made his move long ago. I guess he kind of did make his move and we had both agreed, his moves weren't making the grade. He was a total player. He didn't need the job as my vet tech slash manager. He just did it to piss of his parents. They came from old money and had expected him to take on the family business. Oxford Ronan wasn't the family business type of guy. But what Ox definitely wasn't was interested in me.

"Jesus," Violet sighed. "That man. He was put on this earth to torment me, I swear."

"You're not special, Vi. He makes anyone he comes into contact with feel that way. Quinn is...well, Quinn is especially talented in the art of dickishness."

I maneuvered around a farmer out trying to herd his sheep off the road and inwardly cringed. I'd lived in Ireland for many years, but I still hadn't mastered the art of driving like a local here. You took your life into your hands when you got behind the wheel in this country. Nerves of steel were only my thing in the vet world. On these roads? I just focused on getting from point A to point B.

"So?" I asked her. "What's the verdict? Am I turning around or are you in?"

She didn't look at me, just stared straight ahead. "I'm in. What do I need to know?"

"Too much to cover in the next five minutes. But you should know something." I so didn't want to update her on the Rex and me thing. The fact that I was even thinking there was a Rex and me was ludicrous. However, he was bound to be there as he seemed to be everywhere lately, so she might as well not go in blind.

"Remember that guy from the bar in Galway?"

"The hotty with the hair? Yes. Why?"

"Well, remember how I said he was enemy number one?"

"Yes, I remember. Out with it, Ash."

"He's still enemy number one. No doubt about it. But…" I was hedging. I knew bringing Vi into this was a bad idea, but I was nothing if not consistent in the bad idea department. "Well, I kissed him. Last night. On the lips. At his house."

Her bug eyes almost made me laugh, but this was serious business. "Stop looking at me like that. Your eyes are going to literally pop out of your head. You can't say anything when we see him, okay?"

Her eyes seemed to come out even farther and they were balanced out by the perfect "O" her mouth made. "So, this little trip into the wild. It's to see him?"

"No! No. But…" I might as well just get it all out there. She'd pull it out of me anyway. "It's his horse we're going to help deliver. Also, he has a kid! Can you believe it? Oh, and the kicker is, he still wants to buy up the land. So, yes. Still bad guy number one. Or higher if that was even possible."

"You kissed him? In his house? Last night?" She was broken. I had broken her. Quinn was going to kill me.

"You missed the biggest part, Vi. That man. That, piece of shit, jerk-off, long-hair-loving douchebag actually has a daughter! And she's adorable. And, oh, wait for this. He has a lab. My freaking kryptonite. Kids and labs. I was done before I even knew what was happening. You have to help me, so snap out of it!"

She looked appropriately chastised and I turned into the long lane that would lead to the man who just wouldn't get out of my head. "Okay," she said. "We need a plan. But first, tell me. Is our end goal to bring him closer or banish him to the far reaches of hell?"

"Hell. Definitely hell."

"Okay. I'm on it."

Violet McGregor had been my wing woman for as long as I could remember. We were a team, and obnoxious Rex McDaniel had no idea what he was up against.

I parked the car, grabbed by bag from the back seat and went to deliver a horse. Nothing else. No kissing. No being backed up against a desk and definitely no talking about kids and dogs. Nope. No siree.

We walked into the now familiar stable, still fancier than anything I'd ever seen and went in search of the delivery team since there was no one waiting for us to tell us where we were needed.

I walked into the treatment area where Ox and I had only just been last week and saw they were all there waiting. Including the Lord and Master, Rexford McDaniel III.

"Doctor Murphy. Thanks for coming."

"Zip it fancy pants. Tame your goldilocks and let Ashlyn do what you asked her to do. Preferably from way over there." I turned to look at Vi beside me and nearly burst out laughing at the look on her face. She was gesturing for him to go stand in the stall corner. She looked at me and shrugged her left shoulder. "What? Too much?"

"No. Just right." I burst out laughing. "Nicely done. He might get trampled and ruin his pretty suit, but just right."

Rex stood there eyeing us up like we were two shovels short of a full load while simultaneously pulling that crazy mane of hair of his up and into a quick man-bun with a hair tie he had stowed in his pocket. He then proceeded to roll up the crisp white sleeves of his pristine dress shirt and I momentarily forgot who I was and why I was there. All I knew was that arm porn was real and I was its latest devotee. Damn, the man had fine forearms. Of course he did. Of course God had sent me my arch enemy in the form of this man. It was all those times I'd shown up for church hungover in high school. I knew I'd be paying for those one day. It looked like that day was today.

Days, Ashlyn. Days.

This man wasn't going away any time soon and the sooner I became immune to his ways the better. I wasn't about to let him win.

"Her name is Hazel. This is her first birth and I'm going to kill that son of bitch vet we were supposed to have on staff. You'd think he could have had half a brain and figure out when taking a vacation or quitting or whatever the hell it is that is his current situation, you'd think, Ashlyn, that he had enough care for the animals he'd sworn to protect. Now" —he turned and walked over to the mare—"I assume you have all the"—he looked at Violet with that same single eyebrow raise that had hooked me this morning—"help, you need?"

I felt Violet's elbow jab into my side and I jolted out of the haze I was in. He was standing there, gently whispering to the poor mare in her first labour, sleeves rolled up, all fired up and ready to do battle. I was weak and he was strength. I didn't know how I was going to do this without falling for this man. The one man on earth I simply didn't have the option of falling for. It wouldn't just destroy me. It would destroy my team and my family. The business was everything to them.

I chewed my bottom lip and contemplated my next move. I would obviously have to deliver the foal and then reassess my options. Maybe I would win the lottery tomorrow. Or maybe aliens would take Rex away to their ship and perform mind-altering tests on him. "We've got it from here, Rex. You can go."

"Wouldn't dream of it, princess. I find I quite enjoy watching you in action." He turned to face me and I was sure he could see how flustered I was getting. Damn him again.

Double damn him. "I'm also enjoying watching your adorable face right now."

"I. Am. Not. Adorable. Nor a princess." Somehow those words moved me into action and shook me from my hormonal stupor. "Stay or go. Doesn't matter to me, but stay out of my way."

"I'm here to help, Doctor. You're the boss."

"Ha," I barked out. "Not if you have anything to say about it." I knelt down and started prepping the mare for the birth. Staying focused was what I needed to do now. Get the delivery done. Hope for a smooth birth and pack up and retreat back to my house to plan for another day.

"Violet," I looked up at my best friend to find her smirking and looking between Rex and me. "Can you help me?"

"Sure thing, Ash. Um, how long do you think we'll be here?" She looked up from her phone. "Quinn is somewhat enraged right now."

"Tell Quinn to fuck off. He can go and be enraged with someone else right now. It's what he does best. You're with me for the indefinite future." I looked up at her and saw the worry in her eyes and instantly felt horrible for dragging her down to my miserable level. "Sorry, Vi. If I'm going to be more than a couple of hours, I'll have Ox come and drive you home, okay?"

"It's fine. Quinn can manage the twins. At least, I think he can. He can manage a team of unruly lawyers, right? Surely he can spend a few hours with his children and both of them can survive, right?"

"Good luck with that, Vi. I'll get you back home soon, k?"

"I can take you home," Rex said from somewhere on the other side of the horse. "It's no problem."

I laughed under my breath. Now, that I'd like to see. Quinn "Caveman" Murphy letting some other guy drop his wife off would be totally entertaining. I'd almost leave this birth to watch that. Rex wouldn't know what had hit him. Quinn was ruthless before you factor Violet in. Of course, they weren't married. Violet had zero interest in that, which irritated Quinn to no end, but he still claimed her as his wife. And Violet was the adorable one. Curly red hair, freckles and tiny. Every caveman's dream woman.

Unlike me. Tall, curvy with straight black hair. Plus I'd been told the look on my face, for the most part, terrified men. Might be why I was in the middle of an epic dry spell. Vibrator dates were getting predictable. One day I'd have to figure out how to mix it up with a real, live male specimen.

"Something funny, Ash?" Violet knew where I was heading with my train of thought. I could hear the amusement in her voice.

"No. I think you should definitely take Rex's offer. Kills two birds with the proverbial single stone. I get him off my back for a while and Quinn gets you back earlier than expected. It's a win/win really."

The mare gave a whinny and I knew I needed to focus and get back to work. Daydreaming would have to wait. I smoothed a hand down her side and bent to whisper in her ear. "It's okay now, Hazel. This is how it's gonna go." And I proceeded to tell her every move I made before I made it, zoning out everything but the health of both animals that were now in my care.

CHAPTER ELEVEN

REX

*W*e'd been at it for a while now. At least a couple of hours. I couldn't tell what was wrong but something definitely was. I didn't want to leave Hazel, but I had promised to drive Violet home.

"Ashlyn?" She sat beside the horse, constantly checking various things. Things I had no clue about, but shit, she was incredible. Most of the time, arms deep in the horse, but not panicking. Not letting Hazel feel any stress, even though I hadn't seen a birth take this long before. "Are you going to be okay if I take Violet home now? I imagine her husband is getting worried."

"He's not her husband," came the muffled reply from somewhere underneath the horse's undulating belly.

"Okay, well, whatever he is, it sounds like he'll want her home by now. Especially if there are twins involved."

I could hear the woman in question arguing quietly with Ashlyn's brother off in a corner. Looks like her reprieve was up. "Violet?" I called to her. "I can take you home now."

She looked up from the call and tilted her head to the right taking me in. Assessing me I was sure. She smiled brightly and I could see why Quinn was antsy to get her home. She was a beauty. "Thanks. I think the babies have nearly claimed victory," she said.

"You don't have to do that." I could hear Ashlyn, but couldn't see her inside the cavernous stall. "Quinn should be able to wrangle those two into a car seat by now, for God's sake. Make him come get her."

"It's fine. You're doing fine here and I need to swing home to grab a change of clothes and Miller will be home for lunch soon. Then I'll come back around with her if that's okay? She's on this awful half-day school program. I don't know how any parent can get any work done."

I got no reply, so assumed she was otherwise occupied with the horse. I looked up to see Violet looking at me with her head cocked and a half smile on her face. "So, hotshot, you ready?" she asked.

"Hotshot?"

"If the shoe fits."

I laughed and went in search of my keys, unsure if giving this firecracker a ride home was in my best interests. I had no idea what in the hell I was doing with her friend and it was probably not a good idea to get too close to her self-proclaimed guardian.

"Ash," I heard her call out. "Fabio here is going to give me a ride. I'd rather not have Quinn barging in here with the babies. And yes, I know you're elbow deep in horse vagina and can't say much or drive me yourself and yes, you're stressed that I'll be in close proximity to fancy pants here, but fret not, my friend. All will be well."

"Fancy pants?" I asked. "Let's see. Fancy pants, hotshot and Fabio. Which will it be?"

She smiled and hooked her arm through mine, a move that instantly put me on edge. I didn't do casual familiarity. This woman was an incredible enigma. She went from hot to cold, back to hot and was probably holding cold as my next surprise. Ever since the infuriating Doctor Murphy had come through my doors, nothing made sense.

Only Miller made sense to me these days. Glancing at my watch as I tried to untwist myself from Violet's grasp, I saw that it was definitely time to get moving. I hated being the parent that picked up their kid last. Miller had had enough of feeling abandoned with her mom and so far, I'd kept a stellar track record of being on time when it counted. Even with a tyrant of a father who believed breaks were for the weak. Bringing her into the office every day was becoming a problem, but he could shove it for all I cared.

No response had come from beneath the horse, and I assumed that would be the best I could hope for. "Shall we then?"

"Oh, Fancy Pants it is then. We shall, Mr. McDaniel. Pretty soon we'll be able to hear the wails of my children all the way over the hills. I need to get home to save them from their dad."

I opened her door and shut it before she could come up with a new nickname for me and went around to get in and give this vixen a ride home and mine her for as much information on her best friend as I could in fifteen minutes.

"Don't think I'm giving you any trade secrets, McDaniel. Ashlyn Murphy has been my ride or die since we were sixteen and nothing you or your fancy hair can say could make me divulge her secrets."

"Oh, I'm not after her secrets."

"No?" She started chewing on her bottom lip and narrowed her eyes. "Why give me the ride home then?"

I tried my best to put as bland a look on my face as possible. "I was going this way?"

"Ha! Bullshit. You don't even know me or the man who

will undoubtedly be waiting in the drive when we arrive, wanting to tear you limb from limb. Why risk it?"

I laughed and turned to see if she was being serious. She most definitely was. "Limb from limb? Wow, that's going to be messy."

She threw her head back and laughed as I exited the lengthy drive and finally got onto the highway. "You're something else, Fancy Pants. She certainly has met her match."

"Match?"

"Don't even try to tell me you're not interested. I might be exhausted from my life, but my eyes are working just fine."

"Enlighten me."

"You've been watching her. Not staring, but watching. Secret glances. Little half-smiles. Concerned looks. You're watching out for her."

"I'm watching out for my investment."

"Maybe. But you like her. Admit it."

I stayed silent. I'd been caught in this trap before. It was true, of course. There was something that if I could explore, I would, but this was going to be strictly a business transaction. I needed Ashlyn Murphy to sell me her farm. That was it.

That horrible feeling I'd had the past week started back up again and I mentally threw up a shield. Guilt had no place in this negotiation. I needed Miller to stay with me. The end. Ashlyn would not become a complication, just someone I needed to get on my side. I needed her land. My father actually needed her land, but I needed my father to co-operate and play nice and if the land was what it took until I figured out a way to secure my daughter in Ireland, then land it would be.

"You're awfully quiet," Violet said into the silent void I'd created. "Penny for your thoughts?"

More like two million dollars, the amount I was prepared

to offer Ashlyn for her property. Surely she couldn't refuse. There was a lot of veterinary medicine pro bono work she could do with two million dollars.

"Just lost in the Irish countryside."

She rolled her eyes and I knew I needed to up my game. Undercover agent would never be my career path, that was damn sure.

"Turn here."

"You live beside Ashlyn?"

"Yup. She owns our house. And her brother Aiden and his girlfriend Gray own the original house in between. This property was left to Ashlyn in her parent's will." She turned to fully face me and I knew she was someone more than I had initially given her credit for. "This land is in her blood. It's been in our family for a very, very long time. Ashlyn took it on when her parents died. Think about that when you're taking it away from her."

With that, she smiled, got out and walked towards the man holding on to two baby girls, looking as if he'd very much like to tear me apart. Limb by bloody limb.

CHAPTER TWELVE

ASHLYN

I finally finished up with Hazel and watched as she let nature take hold and nuzzled her new baby girl. I was exhausted and it was still the middle of a work day and it hurt just to think about all the clients I had yet to see.

I pulled off my gloves, walked over to the sinks and started to scrub off the residue of working with all that mess. I vaguely heard the doors open. I wasn't paying much attention. Just thinking about getting packed up and back to my offices.

"Ashlyn!"

I turned just in time to stabilize myself as Miller came racing across the floor, latching herself onto my legs. "Miller! Hi." I crouched down to detach her from my legs, desperately trying not to hurt the little girl's feelings, but needing to stay away from one of the two things Rex possessed that got me every time. Labs and crazy little girls.

"Ashlyn, did you just pull that baby horse out of that mommy horse?"

"I sure did, and now—"

"Do horses have vaginas?"

I barked out a laugh and looked anywhere but at her.

"Miller!" her dad's voice rang out. "What did I tell you?"

She rolled her eyes at her dad. "I know what a vagina is, Dad. It's not a bad word, you know." She grabbed a hold of my damp hand and tried to drag me over to the horse and her baby. "Come on Ashlyn. I'm not scared. Can I pet the baby?"

"Not yet, Miller. Give them some time to bond and for the baby to sort out what just happened to her."

"Oh, okay." Her little face was getting to me just like her dad's. The two of them made quite the team. Every time I was positive I had my defenses solidified, one of them gave me either a lopsided grin or sad, puppy-dog eyes and I was agreeing to things I knew I shouldn't be.

"Well, okay, maybe just a quick peak."

She smiled and I knew I'd been played. I should have known better. I was an aunt to many wily young nieces and nephews. I needed to pull out my A game with this one.

She grabbed my hand and I looked up into her dad's eyes as he crossed our path. Something flickered through his eyes and for a moment had the impulse to reach out and lightly run my fingers down the slight scruff on the side of his face in an effort to calm the storm I could see swirling behind his eyes.

"Mills, babe, we should let the doctor get going, sweetheart. She's doing Daddy a favour by being here. She had to leave her own patients just help me out. I'm sure she needs to get back."

The little girl pouted but immediately let go of my hand. "Okay, Daddy. Sorry, Ashlyn. Maybe I can see the baby tomorrow? Will you be coming back to make sure she's okay?"

"Sure. Same time? Will you be here?"

"You don't have to—" Rex started to say, but I cut him off.

"She's my patient. I'll do a wellness visit and make sure the birth didn't cause any damage. I'll be over a few times until I'm sure she's fine. When's your vet coming back?"

He ran his hand through his hair, something I noticed he did when he was stressed. "The fuck if I know."

"Daddy! Language!"

"Sorry, babe. Ashlyn, I'm not sure when the good vet is set to return. Actually, I'm not even sure where in the hell he is. And yes, Mills, I realize you think hell is a swear word. I'll throw some cash in the jar when I get home." He looked up at me as I was trying, unsuccessfully, to stifle a smile. "The swear jar is nearly full. Cursing's a hard habit to break."

"Not if you try hard enough. That's what you always tell me," Miller replied.

He sighed, grabbed her hand and ushered her down the hall ahead of me. When I caught up, he was bent over listening to her whispering in his ear with a deep frown on his face. I made it to the door and I turned to see him looking at me again. "Everything okay?"

He smiled that kilowatt smile, but I owned the patent on fake smiles. I'd been doling them out my whole life. He couldn't fool me, but I wasn't interested in calling him out on it. That would imply I wanted to know more about him. And I most definitely did not. Nope. No siree.

"Everything's fine, Doctor Murphy. Thanks so much for helping us today. I'll expect you can have your admin team send us the bill as usual. Have a safe drive home please."

He smiled pleasantly, turned with his daughter and disappeared into the offices of the vast farm empire he ran. Weird, I thought to myself. He had certainly turned super formal. I hopped into my SUV and pulled out, heading down the long driveway, trying to put the father-daughter duo out of my head. Permanently.

My phone rang and I saw it was Ox. Not many people

would I take a call from while driving, even with Bluetooth technology. The roads in Ireland could murder you with just a curve, followed by an unexpected single lane in an instant.

"What's up?"

"Where the hell have you been all day?"

"Out on an emergency call. Why?"

"Why? Typically you let your second know when you leave the ship in his command."

Jeez, he was sounding super pissed. And I didn't like it. "Are you okay? Why are you freaking out? This happens all the time."

"Not when you're off galivanting all around with Fabio."

"Ah."

"What's that supposed to mean?" His anger was so confusing. We totally took off on each other all the time. Emergencies happened and we rolled with the punches. "I told Sarah where I was going. What exactly is it you're trying to say?"

"I'm not *trying* to say anything. I'm actually telling you that you've been dropping everything for him a lot lately and I think maybe you're losing your perspective." I could feel his fury through the phone. I pictured him angrily stomping around the barn, probably pissing off everyone and anything that got in his way. Men. I swear if it didn't feel so good having their appendage inside me, I would for certain figure out how to become interested in women.

"Okay, Ox. I'm hanging up before you say something you'll regret. I'll be back in a few. Thanks for handling things while I was out. If that's going to start to be a problem for you, let me know and I'll figure something else out."

"I didn't say it was a problem."

"Didn't you?" I sighed. I didn't have the energy to fight with him. He'd been with me from the beginning and now wasn't the time to anger him. I needed all the help I could get to fight the McDaniels. "Look, Ox. He called. He had an emergency and you know..." I paused trying to get the next part right. Hell, I wasn't even sure I knew why I jumped every time he called, but I needed to figure that out and fast. "You know that I'd do that for anyone in need. So, don't. Don't make this bigger than it really is, okay?"

"Fine." And from across the silence, I could fill in the blanks he wanted me to. "I'll see you when you get here. We've got a lot to run over before you jump back in."

The line went dead and I, not for the first time, thought that hanging up on someone in the era of cell phones was so much less effective than when we had actual phones to bang in someone's ear.

I passed Violet and Quinn's house and wondered what she and Rex had talked about on their ride together and if Quinn had been outside when he had dropped her off. When Quinn was younger, we all did our best to ruffle his feathers. It was so damn fun watching him lose his mind so easily. I couldn't believe he hadn't caught on that if he had just stayed silent, no one would have bothered him.

It looked like Aiden and Gray had gotten out of the city for the weekend. Living right next door to me, I had to pass by their driveway to get to mine. Looked like my peaceful, introverted weekend was about to disappear. Aiden had zero personal space issues and hated to sit still. It was guaranteed I would be dragged over for numerous visits. I just hoped they didn't want to head all the way to the coast to the pub. I really needed to sit and pour over the numbers. I was determined to fight Rex and his dad on the sale of my land.

Even though running the horse farm had become incredibly expensive and their offer was crazy attractive, I would not give in to them. There had to be a way to shuffle the money around so that I could have the farm earning its keep long enough to hold the wolves at bay.

I pulled into my spot and headed into the fray. I went around the back of the main clinic building, heading in the back way so I could avoid the angry mob out front that Beth was trying to wrangle. I slipped on my lab coat and got to work clearing the backlog, totally putting Ox and his crazy rage behind me.

A couple of hours went by and I had moved most of the patients through and couldn't wait to be done for the day. I hadn't even checked my phone to see if Aiden had left me any messages. Walking out, I checked the clock and saw it was nearing 4:45 p.m. I only had one patient left. A lab named, I flipped the chart open, Elsa. Of course it was.

"Long time no see." I looked up from hearing his voice, right into those damn eyes that wouldn't let me be. "Ashlyn?"

"You know they have laws against this kind of stalking, right?" Shaking my head, I knew what I had to do. Get him out of the waiting area before Ox came barging in and said who knew what. "Room number two, please."

Walking past him, I moved to the treatment room and waited for him to follow. Damn, damn, damn. He was still dressed in his sexy as fuck suit, except he had taken off the jacket and rerolled up his sleeves. That damn hair had been pulled back in a loose bun at the nape of his neck. And he was carrying a shaking Elsa. Again. Done. Like. Dinner.

I closed the door behind him and helped him settle the nervous dog up on the examination table. "Rex, what the hell happened? I only left you a few hours ago."

"She was in my office with Miller while I took care of a few things and when I came back, she was shaking like this and Miller was losing her fucking mind."

"Language."

"Sorry."

"That was for Miller. Now, let's see what's up with Princess Elsa here. Did she eat anything unusual?"

"No. I mean, well, I wasn't there and Miller was too upset to get anything out of her. So, shit Ash, I don't know. I don't know what's wrong with her. And yes, here I am, second time in a week asking you to save my damn dog and rescue my horses. I'm well aware how this looks. But please, Christ, save her."

I soothed the lab and began my second exam of the dog in as many days. That was the thing with labs. They got into so much trouble so fast that sometimes it was hard to keep them out of the vet's office. I had my suspicions that she had once again eaten something, but I needed to get some X-rays and bloodwork done before I could be certain what the next steps were. I wasn't set up for small animal surgeries, but Rex's facility could handle it.

"Okay, we need to get her back to your barns, Rex. She needs X-rays and bloodwork and possibly surgery and I don't have an onsite lab or the surgical space we need. But you do. I'll go see if Ox has left for the day. I'll need someone to assist."

He had come around to the other side of the table and was whispering in Elsa's ear and without realizing what I was doing, I covered his hand with mine and gave it a squeeze. "Hey. It's going to be okay. She'll be fine. She's a lab. They're made of stronger stuff than most dogs."

"Look at her, Ashlyn. She's scared. Hell, I'm scared. Usually I know why she's sick, but I wasn't watching her. Fuck, I left her with Mills. What kind of dad does that? Leaves a six-year-old in charge of a crazy dog?" He looked up at me with the scared eyes I'd seen hundreds of times before. Our animals mean more to us than we realize. And it's not until they might be taken away that we typically come to that conclusion.

"It makes you a normal dad, Rex. We don't know what we've got here yet. So, let's wait and see and then we can decide on our course of action, okay? Is Miller still at your offices?"

"No, Maisie took her home when she saw how freaked out I was. Maisie's my assistant. She'll stay with her overnight. She's got a granddaughter the same age. Miller loves it there."

"Okay, good. Things may get worse before they get better. I'll be right back and we'll head back to your space. If you could call ahead and see if the techs could hang around? I'll need some lab testing help if that's okay."

"If they've left, they'll come back."

"No, no need to force them to do anything. I'll figure it out. Don't make them come back on a Friday afternoon."

He looked at me like the businessman I first met, raised an eyebrow daring me to say any more on the matter and then went back to soothing his dog. I went to find Ox only to find my clinic had become a ghost town. It was normal for Sarah to lock up while I was in with a last patient, so I went over the barns to see if I could find my errant manager.

I searched everywhere and asked any staff who I came upon, but to no avail. The slippery shithead had escaped without answering for his anger earlier. I'd have to deal with him later. I grabbed my travel bag, scooped up as much as I could from my supplies and met Rex back in the exam room.

"Okay, let's take my Rover. It's got the space in the back where we can lay her down. Ready?" He looked frantically at me and I was completely unsettled. This strong, egotistical, controlling man wasn't jelling with the man standing in front of me. This man was human, emotional and vulnerable. "No, you're not ready." I put down my bag and glanced at the dog. She looked at me with those sad eyes. The eyes that knew she'd gone one step too far this time. I put my hands on either side of his face and looked him in the eyes. "Hey, Rex." He blinked. "As much as I hate to admit it, I'm going to need jackass Rex to come back and help me out here. My team appear to have taken their leave for the weekend and I can't do this alone. Got it?"

He snapped out of whatever place he'd gone and gave me a nod. We were back in business. "Okay, I'm just going to run out to the car to get it ready for her. Then I'll need you to carry her and settle her in. Be right back."

CHAPTER THIRTEEN

REX

I missed the heat from her hands as soon as she turned and left to go prepare the rover for Elsa. Fuck. How would I ever explain to Miller that the only thing holding her together here in Ireland had died in my arms? Ashlyn needed to hurry the hell up.

I turned and gave Elsa a little nuzzle. "Come on girl. Don't do this to me. We're a team. I need you. Miller needs you. The three of us? We're a family. Ireland doesn't work without you here. Do. Not. Die. You hear me?"

Ashlyn rushed back in and signaled it was time to go. I gently scooped up Elsa, wincing as she whimpered from the movement, and followed Ashlyn out the door. Thank God for her. I knew I was going to all sorts of hellish places for how I was manipulating her, but this was honest to goodness need. I needed her to pull us through on this one. If anyone could save this dog, it was Doctor Ashlyn Murphy.

We settled Elsa in the rear of her SUV, where Ashlyn had folded down a seat so I could sit beside the dog and keep her steady. We took off and I tried to hold on, but it seemed Ashlyn was in a bigger hurry than she had let on.

"Slow down. You're throwing me all over the place back here."

"You want the dog to live?" I stared her down.

"Of course."

"Then this is how fast we're driving. Sit down and hold onto her. That's your only job over the next ten minutes. Did you call ahead?"

"They'll be there."

She looked me back in the eye, always challenging me. "You're sure?"

"I said they'd be there, so they'll be there. Got it?"

She backed down and kept her eyes on the road and I felt like a royal ass. She didn't deserve me yelling at her. She had dropped everything, again, to help me out and all I could do was snap at her. But I could be excused for being a little irrational. Anything could be used against me at this point in my custody situation. The amount of money that Miller was worth would always be attractive to my ex. Besides the fact that this dog had unknowingly grown on me and she was currently Miller's world. Ashlyn could take it.

We rode in strained silence until the farm came into view. This was a first. I'd never been thankful for my dad having such a huge operation until this very moment. His state-of-the-art, overpriced and overrated clinic was now my favourite place on earth. I'd probably get a bill for the overtime I'd made the techs work, but it didn't matter. I'd cross the bridge my father would surely build when the time came for it. Right now, I needed this dog to live.

We parked and I hopped out to carry Elsa back out of the trunk. I couldn't help but notice she'd gone a bit more limp. "Hurry, Ashlyn. She's getting worse."

She opened the door for me and I led her down the same hall we'd only travelled out of a few hours ago into the testing area of the clinic. I gently laid Elsa down on the x-ray table and turned to watch Ashlyn slipping on her rubber exam gloves.

"What can I do?"

"Follow my instructions." Even through all of this stress, I still took a minute to appreciate all that was Doctor Ashlyn Murphy in her scrubs, giving me orders, talking to the vet techs who had arrived back on site. In her element, she was the perfect mix of woman and doctor in charge.

"Okay, we're going to draw some blood, then X-rays and then we'll have some answers. Hopefully."

She got to work shaving Elsa where she would need to draw the blood, deftly preparing the dog.

"Hold her still, please."

I moved to the opposite side and leaned over the shaking dog while Ashlyn drew her blood.

"Okay," Ashlyn said. "That's done. Now, we x-ray." She handed the vials off to the tech, gave them some instructions and then started to position the x-ray machine to where she wanted it. "Calm her while I move her around for the pictures, okay?"

"Yeah, sure. Got it."

She looked at me while chewing her bottom lip, looking concerned. "What?"

She smiled a sad smile and my stomach dropped. "She's going to be okay. I'm going to have a look in her stomach and see if I can figure out what went in there to make her feel this way and then get it out. Routine for labs. If it's anything else, the bloodwork will tell us. Now, hold her still while I drape you."

"I don't need it." She was coming at me with a heavy looking apron made of lead to protect me from the harmful rays. "Just get on with it."

"I don't cut corners. Put it on or get out. Your choice."

She stood there, arms crossed, eyebrow raised, waiting

for me to fall in line. She was right. I didn't want a vet who cut corners. "Fine. Give it to me." She slipped the apron over my head and left me to go finish the X-rays.

A few clicks later and we were standing around the results. "Ah. There it is."

I narrowed my eyes at the screen, but all I could make out were black and white blobs in various spots inside of Elsa. "There what is? What are we looking at?"

"Slow your roll. I can see where our problem is and I've got good news and bad news. Which would you like?"

"Why don't you just tell me all the news, instead of trying to be cute." God I was an ass.

"I'm going to let your lousy attitude slide only because I asked you to be this way, but know that I don't tolerate this kind of shit inside my operating room. Because that's where we're headed next. You can thank your luck stars you've got loads of cash and this here fancy surgical suite."

"Oh? And why's that?"

"Because your dog needs surgery."

"Surgery? Why?" Shit, that sounded scary. Miller was going to kill me.

"Because"—she pointed to a greyish black mass—"whatever this is, it's blocking her intestinal tract and by the look of it, she didn't just eat it. It's been there for a day or so."

Relief flooded me. "So it didn't happen today when she was inside my office?"

"Nope. Whatever this is, I'd say it's been trying to move through her body for at least 24 hours, but probably more like 34 to 48 hours. It's made its way fairly extensively, but now it's stuck and possibly wrapped around her intestinal tract, restricting the healthy flow. I'll need to go in and extract whatever it is."

"You can't tell what it is from the X-ray?"

"No. Of course, it would be ideal if I knew what she'd

ingested, but we'll take this one slow. So, I'm just going to find the lab results and then we can get started. Be right back."

She disappeared behind the lab door and I pulled out my phone to call Miller and give her an update.

The phone rang and my girl answered right away. "Daddy?" Her little voice started to wobble and I had to hold myself together. It was us against the world. I could not afford to let her know I was just as scared as she was.

"Mills. She's going to be fine, okay?"

"I want to come see her, Daddy."

"Not right now, Miller. I promise you, she's fine. She's going to have a little bit of a surgery to take out whatever it was she ate and then she'll be all sorted out, okay babe?"

She sniffled and I knew she was holding back the floodgate. "Daddy? Isn't surgery cutting her open? Is she gonna die?"

"Hey, babe. I've got Doctor Murphy looking after Elsa. You know she won't let anything bad happen to her, right?"

"Ashlyn is Elsa's doctor again?" I could hear her smile over the phone. "Is she going to cut her open to find what's hurting her?"

"Yes, she definitely is, so, you've got nothing to worry about, right? Doctor Murphy is the best." I looked up to see the doctor in question appear through the door and raise her eyebrows in answer to my proclamation. "Mills? Honey?"

"Yes, Daddy?"

"I've got to go, okay? I've got to help Doctor Murphy with Elsa. I'll call you when she's done. Go have some fun."

"I'll try, Daddy. Love you."

Right in the fucking heart. With the sharpest arrow. This dog could not die today. "Love you too, babe. The mostest mostest mosest you've ever been loved."

"I love you more. Infinity plus those mostests."

This was the game we always played when we had to say goodbye to each other, even if it was just to go to sleep.

"You win."

"Yessss," her little whisper came across the phone. "Bye, Dad."

I tucked the phone away and slipped off my suit jacket. Gathering up my hair, I tied it up, rolled up the sleeves on my dress shirt a little higher and prepared for my first surgery assist.

CHAPTER FOURTEEN

ASHLYN

*D*amn, if I wasn't so busy saving his damn dog's life again, I'd take a moment to appreciate all that was Rexford McDaniel the Third standing there in front of me. Perfect navy suit pants, molded to his freaking perfect body. Fitted white dress shirt, now exposing those forearms that I was sure could chop wood or sign multi-million dollar deals all day. And that hair. I never thought I was a hair woman, but apparently, I just hadn't run my hands through the right head of hair yet.

Focus, Murphy, I told myself. Daydreams could come later, when there was easy access to the new vibrator I'd just scored on Prime Day. Who knew Amazon carried such a diverse selection of sex toys and put them on sale a couple times a year? Amazon Prime, a great imagination and this man standing here in front of me was all I needed tonight.

I smirked and walked over to the sink to scrub up. "Wash up, McDaniel. You're solo assisting me with this."

"Where are the lab techs I paid to be here?"

"One of them really needed to go pick her daughter up

and the other one isn't getting near this dog. So, wash up. I need your help."

He smiled and joined me over at the sinks where we proceeded to scrub our hands. I had changed into a clean pair of scrubs and turned to look at his pristine outfit and knew he needed to do something about that.

"You have any scrubs around here?" I asked him.

"Ah," he looked around, "no? Maybe? I don't know."

I spied a packaged gown on a shelf and grabbed it and threw it at him. "Put this on. We need to be sterile and that outfit needs to stay white if at all possible."

He looked down at his shirt and shrugged. "This gown isn't going to save my shirt. Hang on." And he proceeded to quickly unbutton said shirt and I whipped around, making myself busy trying to find the medicine I'd need to knock Elsa out. "I wouldn't have pegged you for the shy type, Doc."

Still avoiding looking anywhere near his direction, I laughed awkwardly. "You have no idea, McDaniel. I'm as introverted as they come."

"All done. You can turn around."

"I wasn't—"

"You were."

I felt my cheeks heat up and if there wasn't an animal in need I would have wished for a hole to open up and swallow me. "Let's just get started."

"Look at me."

"What?" I looked up sharply, trying very hard to focus on his eyes and not the wide expanse of lightly dusted chest hair roving across the hardest chest I think I'd ever seen. These gowns were entirely too see-through.

"If you're avoiding looking at me, you're going to fuck this up. So, get your fill and then we can move on."

"Arrogant ass."

"There's my girl."

111

We both looked at each other, unable to break free of the endearment that had just tied us together for a brief moment. I cleared my throat and focused the surgical lights in the area I wanted and checked to make sure Elsa was fast asleep.

I would have to do the job of a few people and I'd need Rex to help. I hoped to God he wasn't squeamish. I risked a look up into his eyes. "Are you going to be able to do this? I'd try to find Ox, but I'd like to get this moving along."

He looked at me with the clinical, cold eyes I remembered from our first meeting. "I'm fine. Let's get this done."

"Okay, first I'll need to shave the area and then sterilize it before I can get in there to see what's going on." I passed him a pair of rubber gloves and got down to business. Elsa was prepped and we were ready to go in only a few minutes. Holding the knife, I paused before cutting her open and looked up into his eyes. They'd melted into pools that reflected what he must be feeling at this moment. Owners were always this way. Nonchalant about their pet until they were faced with their mortality.

"Rex?" He blinked and looked back at me. "She's going to be fine. I'm really quite good at this."

He relaxed and we fell into an intense silence. I wasn't one of the doctors who preferred a noisy environment. No music. No talking. I focused best when silence was present. I asked him for help when I needed it and I had no idea how he was truly faring seeing the insides of his dog.

For the most part, he was a good assistant. He didn't speak unless I asked him a question, he stood still and didn't seem squeamish. "Ah, there you are you little shit." I'd found the blockage and the reason Elsa was so sick.

Carefully grabbing a hold of the bundle, I pulled it out of the dog's intestines and held it up for inspection. "Oh my God!"

I raised my eyes to meet Rex's but found him staring at

the offending blob with the reddest cheeks I'd ever seen. "Is that—?" he croaked out.

"Sure looks like it, doesn't it?"

"Fuck me. Damn it Elsa. You've been in my room."

I put the expensive looking lace thong that was now most definitely ruined, in the dish next to the operating table and shook my head. Of course his dog had women's lacey panties in her intestinal tract. How appropriate.

"I can't fucking believe this."

"Well, wouldn't be the first time a lab's been attracted to, um…"

"Go ahead, Doctor Murphy. Say it." Oh, that was rich. He'd kissed me. Kissed me when he had some other woman's undies living under his bed. Of course, I had no right to any part of him, but it still pissed me off. I guess I had the panties to thank for reminding me that I needed to steer clear of him.

"Nope. Just because labs are attracted to rank smells, doesn't mean anything in this situation, Mister McDaniel."

"Come on."

"No, you come on. You're such a lying piece of shit. Did you kiss me the minute after she'd left or did you give it a day."

"Not fair, Ashlyn. I didn't mean to kiss you."

I was speechless. I began to close Elsa and wished again for a large hole to appear and swallow me up. "I see."

"No, I don't think you do."

"I do Rex. Message received. Loud and clear. Let's just get Elsa sewed up and home to rest, okay?"

He sighed, loudly and heavily and I got back to work. This was good. Just what I needed. I kept forgetting who I was dealing with here and the universe was kind enough to continue to remind me, each time getting a little louder until my ears were ringing with the reminders of what a colossal dick he was.

I finished the last stitch and ripped off my gloves and apron. "Ashlyn, please."

I dug around in my bag for some pain relievers for the dog and wished I'd brought some along for myself. Ignoring him seemed to be the easiest route to getting out of here with some of my dignity in place.

"Ashlyn. Look at me."

Thankfully the dog chose to move towards consciousness at that moment and I lurched over to the table to check on her. "Hi, sweetheart. How're you feeling? You had a nasty pair of panties all tied up inside your intestines. Who knows what kind of disease might be at this very moment developing inside of you. Doctor Murphy is going to give you some yummy treats that will make sure that disease doesn't take hold, okay? Oh and a nice, big nasty old cone so you don't destroy my handywork."

"Give me a break," came from somewhere behind me. "Come on, Ashlyn. You know what I meant."

I turned with the antibiotics, cone and pain pills ready for him. "As soon as you get her home, crush these up in some peanut butter and get her to take them. One of each, every four hours for the first twenty-four hours, then the pain pills on an as-needed basis. The antibiotics, continue that way until they're gone." I turned back to my bag to start packing up.

"I'm not a saint, Ashlyn. And all I meant was that I didn't know I'd need you to come over and I didn't know that when you did I would be unable to resist the need to kiss you, okay? So knock it off and look at me for a minute."

"It's fine, Rex. I'm fine. Your dog is going to be fine. But keep an eye on her over the next few days and you'll need to find a vet for a follow-up visit. I can give you the name of a couple of good ones in the area if your vet hasn't returned from wherever the hell he is by then."

"Stop. I don't need a different vet. I have you."

I angrily zipped up my bag and swung to look him in the eye like he'd been waiting for. "You do not have me. Not in any way, shape or form. I'm done rescuing you. Find a new vet to drive insane. You have a lab. Keep an eye on her. They eat anything, even gross dirty panties." I swung the bag on my shoulder and fished my keys out. "I'll get one of your staff to come help you carry her to whatever vehicle you'll use to get her home. You need to keep her still for an hour and don't let her walk or lick the stitches. Make sure she's wearing the cone or else she'll lick the area raw and open the incision."

I walked to the door, not letting him get a word in edge-wise. "Remember, pills when you get home and every four hours. Call my office if you can't find a vet for her follow-up."

And with that, I walked out the door before I totally lost any dignity I had remaining and beat him over the head with my medical bag.

CHAPTER FIFTEEN

REX

J walked into our offices Monday in the foulest of moods and hoped everyone was able to figure out that today wasn't their day to ask me for a goddamn thing. I'd spent the weekend nursing Elsa the panty-thieving lab and dealing with a very emotional and needy six-year-old. Add to that I still was no closer to getting Ashlyn Murphy to sell her land to me and I was quickly running out of time.

My father didn't make threats lightly and he probably had already called my ex to tell her to come and get Miller and take me back to the States. I refused to be banished to corporate suburbia. I liked it here and here is where we were staying. I just had to figure out how to get Ashlyn to sell me the land that was her everything and convince my father I was the son he had always wanted and not the disappointment he currently thought I was.

I was royally fucked on both goals.

I sat down at my desk and spun my chair around in circles like a child, desperately trying to come up with some sort of plan to get back in Ashlyn's good graces. I just needed an in and I could blast open her damn locked-up-tight heart.

What were the chances that damn dog would find the last woman I'd slept with's panties? I didn't even know they were in the house, for Christ's sake. If I could remember her name I'd figure out a way to send them back to her straight out of the garbage from the clinic. That little stunt might have cost me everything.

A knock sounded at the door and I briefly debated ignoring it, but I knew I had more than just this land deal to work on. Better to bury myself in a mountain of paperwork than drown my sorrows sitting alone in my dark office brooding over being surrounded by women who hated me, including my dog who looked at me like I had actually stuffed the undies down her throat.

"Come in."

"Rex."

Ah, Jesus. Could I seriously not catch a break? My father never knocked, sneaky bastard. I fought the desire to hide under my desk and looked him in the eye, daring him to test me today.

"Dad. What can I do for you?"

"You can tell me you've signed the deal to purchase that land I wanted, for starters."

Of course that's what he came for. "Why is it so important to you to have that land in particular?"

He raised an eyebrow and tilted his head. "It's land. I want it because it neighbours our farms and then we can build the expansion. What in the hell is so hard to understand about that, boy? You know this."

"Boy?"

"You heard me, Rexford. You promised me last week you'd get this done and just like always, you're unable to close this deal. You have forty-eight hours and then I'll find someone else who can get the job done and you can prepare for your transfer back to the States." He leaned over my desk and I could feel his hot, disgusting breath on mine. It appeared dear old Dad still liked to start his day with a little whiskey. "Get me that land and we won't have a problem."

He slammed his hands on the desk as he pushed off and I slowly unclenched my fists. I fucking hated my father most of the time, but right now, I wished he would drop dead from whatever was the most painful disease known to man. What kind of parent gave his only child an ultimatum to destroy someone in order to keep his daughter and because he "wanted it"?

I picked up the closest object, some sort of ridiculous paper weight, and threw it at the now closed door. It bounced off and hit the floor, taking a piece of the door with it. Shit. That didn't make me feel any better. And now I had to deal with how to fix the damn door.

I grabbed my suit jacket and just like *Groundhog Day*, stormed through my offices to go convince Doctor Ashlyn Murphy to give me the one thing she was never going to want to. I guess it was time to swallow any last piece of dignity I had left. I would need to do whatever it took to get her to let her guard down and convince her to sell out to me, possibly even tell her the truth of it all.

I felt sick to my stomach but there was no way out that I could see. I needed to keep Miller here with me, far away from her poor excuse for a mother. It had to be done and it looked like there would be more than just one casualty. I'd probably never be the same after I became the very thing I'd sworn as a kid I'd never be. Someone who did anything to seal the deal.

I was slowly becoming dead inside. Anything for the deal. Even family were expendable. And friends. Whether she would admit it or not, we were friends. And if she ever found out who I really was, there'd be no hope for us to stay that way.

I pulled into her drive, again, and parked, giving myself a minute to figure out how me barging in here kept happening and what she was going to do about this visit. One thing was for sure. Ox, wouldn't be too excited to see me again. It was clear to everyone but Ashlyn that he was crazy in love with her and anyone who appeared to be competition was on his shit list.

I got out, put on my jacket and tamed the wild mane as I pulled open the door to the office of the woman who I desperately needed to see things my way.

"Rex! How nice to see you again. How's Elsa?" her receptionist asked.

"She's doing well, thanks. Ah, how is Doctor Murphy's day looking? Is there any time in her schedule for a new appointment?"

She scanned her computer, looking to see what, if anything, was available. I leaned over the counter and flashed her my best smile, hoping it worked as well on her as it usually worked on the women I flashed it to.

"Ah, yes, yes. I think I can fit you in later today if that works?"

"Sure. What time?"

"At the end of her day, so 4:45?"

That fit nicely into my plan. Another end of the day rendezvous. "4:45 it is then. I'll see you later, Sarah."

"Sure, can I tell her what it's for? Elsa need a check-up already?"

"Nope. Just tell her I'll see her then. Thanks."

She looked at me quizzically and I smiled again. She softened and I turned to go before the doctor got wind that I was there. I wanted this meeting to be a sneak attack and an end of the day time slot was just the thing I needed to get it done.

I got back into my car and took off to go check on the farm before heading home to get Miller and Elsa occupied for the night with Maisie. I wasn't planning on coming home until I'd gotten those papers signed, even if it took all night.

CHAPTER SIXTEEN

ASHLYN

I glanced at the clock on the wall of the clinic and thanked God my day was almost over. I'd spent the weekend alternating between worrying about Elsa the panty-eating wonder lab and fending off questions from my siblings about why I was in such a foul mood. I was exhausted. I was the last single Murphy standing, unless you counted our great-aunt Carol who'd never found "the one." We all knew she was not into men, at all, but kept up the front for her secret because it was useless to try to encourage her at the ripe old age of eighty-two that dating a woman might be just what the doctor ordered.

I knew I had one last patient and then I had a hot date with my couch and a beer. A bag of chips would be dinner and possibly I'd throw in a hot bath to close out the evening.

"Okay," I patted the bouncing head of the puppy up on the table. "He's all good. Shots are in and you're good to go. We'll see him back in when he's due for the next round."

"Thanks, Doctor."

I followed them out of the exam room, dropped their

chart on Sarah's desk and picked up the last patient's chart, not bothering to open it up.

"Hey, Ash," Sarah said. "Mind if I head out? I've got to go pick up the kids and all is done here. I'll lock up on my way out."

"Yeah, sure. See you tomorrow." I was totally distracted and not really in the mood to point out that this was pretty much her routine on the daily. Today, I just wanted to be done so I could begin the not thinking part of my evening.

"Knock, knock." I knocked on the alternate exam room door, looked up into those damn freaking eyes and stopped cold. "What in the hell are you doing here? Again!"

Rex McDaniel. The bane of my existence. Sitting there inside my exam room, again, with his sexy as hell grey suit, worn brown dress shoes and that hair, distracting me from my anger...again.

He got up and I held my hands out, trying to stop his advance. "Stay. Over there." I waved in the general direction from which he had come. "Seriously, this is getting to be a problem. What in the hell is wrong now? Did the referrals I gave you all fall through?"

He stood there, staring at me with the strangest look on his face. Like, a mix of anger, heat and resignation. "Has something happened?" I asked him again. "You're just standing there and it's freaking me out. Please, for God's sake, say something."

He said nothing, of course, but continued to move forward into my space, forcing me to back up until I hit the door behind me. "Oh no, buddy. Not gonna happen. One kiss, that was it and we both agreed it wouldn't happen again. I see that look in your eyes. Back the fuck up."

He stopped and seemed to snap out of it, backing up a step to give me space. I crossed my arms over my chest and pursed my lips. "I mean it Rex. I'll knee your precious jewels so hard you won't walk straight for a week. Back up!" He tilted his head and took two steps back, still not saying a word.

"Why are you here? Why? Is this some kind of torture devised to get me to give in to your father? Why do you keep coming back here? Why aren't you saying anything?"

God, I was losing touch with reality. I needed to take a deep breath, focus and get him out of there. Unfortunately, or fortunately, he chose that moment to smile his disarming smile. The one I kept getting caught up in. "Elsa is fine, Ashlyn. She's actually with Miller at my assistant's place for the night getting waited on hand and foot, I'm sure. I didn't come here for Elsa."

"Oh," I whispered. "Then why did you come here?"

He slowly came back towards me and I had the feeling I was being stalked. Slow, deliberate steps headed back in my direction. He stopped in front of me and I tried to take a step backwards, only to come back up against the damn door again.

"You," he said.

"Me?" I squeaked out.

"Yes, Ashlyn Murphy. I came here for you."

"Oh," I whispered.

"Yes, oh." He leaned one hand against the door beside my head and then the other hand followed to the other side. "So, I came here with plans, but it looks like those plans might not be the plans I'm going to go with."

"Plans?" Dear Lord. What had happened to me? I sounded like I'd lost my damn mind. My mind had nothing to do with what I was feeling, though. The land down under was suddenly in control and she'd been on extended leave for so long, she was pretty rusty.

Wait a second, what in the hell was I doing? This man was the enemy and I'd spent the entire weekend reminding myself of that and fortifying the walls I needed to build to keep him out. I closed my eyes and took a breath in, through my mouth because, damn, the man always smelled so divine and it made me weak.

"No."

"No?" he said.

"No plans. I'm not doing plans with you, Rex. We've already discussed this. You"—I opened my eyes and looked him head on, ignoring the deep blue sea that would take you in and make you fall in love with it—, "are not someone who I make plans with. You want to take away my plans and give me back your own. I can't let that happen, so, no. No plans."

"No plans," he echoed.

"Nope. No plans. Now, if you'll excuse me—"

His lips descended on mine and I drew in a quick breath, knowing it might be my last for a few minutes. Damn, the man had plans and I guess they included kissing me sense-less. Every single stupid wall I thought I had built came crashing down with this kiss. He was a freaking master kisser. Of course he was. The damn man was in control of everything, why not his ability to kiss?

His tongue played with my lips, slowly testing my defenses, looking for the weak points where it could slip past and take over. Meanwhile, one of his hands had slipped down off the door and was currently skimming over my T-shirt, making the fabric spark with electricity as his fingers slid down to find my own and entwine with them.

My free hand reacted by claiming the ass I'd wanted to grab a hold of for so damn long and yes, it was like coming home. That hand grabbed a hold and dug in for whatever adventures were coming its way. I might have been weak, but I was beyond caring.

His lips left my mouth and slowly, hungrily explored my

neck, licking and sucking their way down towards my shoulder.

"God, Ashlyn," he sighed into my neck. "You are everything."

I knew what he was talking about. We'd both been avoiding this exact thing for so long, that it was inevitable it would be this good when it finally happened. Anticipation had made us wild with need, disguised as anger. The problem was, was I interested in having it happen? I felt like only bad things would come from giving over to this man. This man who was right now holding my head with both hands so he could gain the traction he needed to access every part of my mouth. All I could do at this moment was plaster both hands flat against the door and try like hell to hold on.

I made the hormonally driven decision to just give in. I was tired, and resisting this man was wearing me down. I'd deal with the fallout when it came. What he was offering me right now was so much more appealing than continuing the fight for the upper hand.

"Babe?"

Oh Jesus, Mary and Joseph. No one in my life had ever dared call me babe. I wasn't the "babe" type, but just now? I was pretty sure I'd lost my panties when he said it. I'd just become that girl.

"Yes?"

"Is there somewhere we could go?"

I tried to find some sense of where and who I was and think straight for one minute. I opened my eyes and looked around. "The table."

He pulled back and I pouted. Oh God, I pouted. Fuck the man, but the innocent little girl act had to stop. "Are you sure?" he asked.

I was sure. Instead of answering, I pushed back from the door, dislodging him from my body, took off my lab coat, tore off my top from the hem and undid the flimsy tie at the side of my basic scrub pants. There was nothing I could do about the utilitarian undies and mismatched bra. There was no time for regrets, only moving forward. Ashlyn Murphy 2.0 had arrived.

He smiled and I moved in, took ahold of his waist and swung him around so I now had my back to the exam table. I'd had enough. It was time for me to just give in for once. "You've got too many clothes on."

I quickly shoved my hands under his jacket to help him slide it off, where it landed in a heap on the floor. He produced a hair tie and pulled back his hair, tying it back like an expert. Next his shirt joined his suit jacket on the floor and he stood there in front of me in all his glory. A light dusting of hair across a well-toned chest cut with muscles layered over each other all the way down to the zipper on his pants.

"Like what you see?"

"Arrogant ass."

He threw his head back and roared with laughter. "You got that right, babe." He stilled and looked at me. Really, truly saw me and I suddenly became incredibly uncomfortable. "God you're beautiful. Come here."

I blushed and leaned into his body letting my skin feel his. I was electric and reacted like a switch had been flipped. Our mouths fused again and he grabbed my hips, effortlessly lifting me onto the exam table. Which was now going to be awfully hard to look at tomorrow.

He fit himself between my open legs and reached around to undo my bra, while delivering butterfly soft kisses just above my breasts and intentionally not getting to the good part, I was sure.

My bra went flying and I gave up fighting the restrain I was holding on to. I attacked his zipper while his lips met back up with mine. After a few seconds of ridiculous fumbling on my part, I finally got his pants down and without hesitation, reached into his boxer briefs to get my eager hands on the goods. And good it was. His impressive cock was rock hard and happy to be released from its confines.

He groaned and I reveled in the newfound power I was experiencing. I grabbed a hold and slowly followed the length down to the tip and gave a slight squeeze. "Fuck, Ashlyn. I'm going to need you to slow down. You'll find it hard to believe, but this actually wasn't the plan," he whispered with his head buried once again in the junction between my shoulder and neck. "When I take you for the first time, it's not going to be on the narrowest possible bed known to man. But if you don't stop that, I'm going to lose what little self-control I have left."

I smiled and went in for a second tug on his hard length. There was going to be some sort of resolution to this conflict. Neither one of us was leaving this room without being fully satisfied with the results.

"I see. It's going to go that way then, is it? Lift up, babe." He grabbed the edge of my panties and tugged them down as I lifted my body up. He flung them behind him with an evil grin on his face and I died a thousand deaths. Things down south were not ready for entertaining. "Stop overthinking. Whatever thought just came into your gorgeous head needs to turn around and leave."

"I'm not, well," Jesus, this encounter had just taken a turn into embarrassing town.

"What? Babe, tell me."

"Are you really that dense? I haven't had any visitors to the southern regions in a very, very long time. Things are a little, well, um, wild down there." I slapped my hands over my face and wished for some semi-dire emergency to find me. My pager was always going off when I was relaxing, so why not now?

"Ashlyn." He gently pried my hands from my face. "Look at me."

I cemented my eyes closed, going by the age-old adage that if I can't see it, it isn't happening.

I was focused on his soft lips brushing against my chin, so when I felt a finger gently exploring the southern region, so it took me by complete surprise. "Oh, no. No, no—"

"Stop freaking out," he whispered. "Relax. There is no way I'm stopping and you've never looked hotter." He continued his explorations, both with his lips and fingers. "Do you know how many times I've thought about this exact moment? This exam room. That lab coat. Those very scrubs on the floor."

Oh God, that felt nice. His fingers continued their in and out motion, his thumb had found home and I was losing this game of wills. It was time to fully give in to his peer pressure and let him take control. "Really?" Was that my voice? I was certainly not the breathy type of girl. Admittedly, there hadn't been anyone who'd ever really rocked my world, sex-wise. This was uncharted territory. Who knew what other new things I'd discover about myself when I was this incredibly turned on?

His lips were back on mine for only a moment, his tongue darting in for a series of quick plunges, mirroring his fingers. "It was getting hard to focus when you were around. I kept wondering how I'd lure you into one of the exam rooms at the stables."

I arched my head back when a particularly intense pulse flew from my clit, ricocheting all over my body. He took advantage of my distracted state and latched onto one of my nipples, tugging it fully into his mouth, again, pulling in perfect harmony with his thumb and fingers.

"Come on, babe. Let it go."

Easy for him to say. He wasn't fully naked inside his offices, laid completely bare for anyone to see. "Mmmm."

"That's it." He picked up the pace and I could feel the pleasure rising, swirling a frantic path through my entire body. My climax was coming on like a freight train and there was nothing I could do but hold on and enjoy the ride.

He moved to the other nipple, giving it the same attention and tweaked the sensitive tip of the one he left behind. I arched into his talented hands and knew he was ruining me for any other, just with a simple touch of his fingers. The man was not-surprisingly talented.

And then it happened. "Jesus Christ." I threw my head back again, arched fully into him and clamped down on his magic fingers, deciding to never let them leave my body. I grabbed hold of his shoulders and held on for dear life, riding the wave of the climax he'd given me, deciding this constituted my workout for the night, my muscles were so engaged.

I slowly relaxed and lifted my head back to its rightful position, opening my eyes to find a very proud peacock staring back at me. "Hi, gorgeous. Shit, you're hot when you come."

I hung my head in embarrassment. I'd never been a vocal girl in the sheets and something wild and wanton had definitely come over me. "Sorry."

I felt his hand on my chin, pushing it up until my head was back to its original position. "Do not, ever again, say that word to me. Are we clear?" His eyes were hard and flickered with angry sparks. "Ashlyn?"

"But—"

He kissed me, hard and angrily. "Enough. There's one thing you should know, babe. I say what I mean and I mean what I say. If I've said it, you can rest assured I meant it. I think you're wildly hot. In your scrubs, on a horse, covered in animal goo. Doesn't matter. And when you let me see the real you. The one you keep well hidden from everyone else? I was done." He pushed his body into my space as far as he could, connecting our bodies, skin to skin. "Fucking hot, got it?"

I sat there silently wondering how in the past thirty minutes this man had gotten past all my hard-earned defenses and turned everything I thought I knew about him upside down. All I could possibly do was nod my head and hope this wasn't the end. My stomach rumbled loud enough to wake the babies at Quinn and Vi's house and I found myself blushing yet again. Thinking back, I guess I'd been too busy and too preoccupied to eat today.

He smiled and brushed a stray hair out of my eyes. "Hungry? Want to get some dinner?"

"Wait, what about y—"

"I can wait," he said. "But that rumbling stomach of yours probably can't. It seems quite insistent we feed it."

I threw my head on his shoulder and groaned. "What were you saying about me being 'fucking hot'? I can't think of anything sexier than a woman whose stomach proclaims its urgent need to eat right after climaxing and before you complete the mutually beneficial part of our encounter."

He did up his pants and pulled me in for a hug. He was a hugger? What in the hell was happening? Had I really pegged him all wrong? Was he really not the asshole I had always thought he was?

He moved around the room, gathering the pieces of my clothing that had gotten scattered around in my haste to get laid in my offices. I hopped down off the table and quickly began the awkward process of redressing as we both set ourselves to rights.

Now came the painful moment when real life started to

intrude into whatever it was we were doing. "Look," I started to say. "You don't have to do this. You probably have somewhere else to be, doing all the, um, things, that you do, and stuff."

"All the things I do and stuff? Yes, you're very right. I do have all those things to do, but I always have time to eat. And Miller and the dog are gone for the night, remember? And I find myself, for the first time since I've come to Ireland, with an entire free night. Nowhere to be. No 'things' to do. Except eat, with you, of course. And interrogate you. So, let's get to it, then, shall we? Where should we go?"

"All night?" I raised an eyebrow.

He smirked back. "All night."

I smiled. "I know just the place. I just need to change. I'll drive, so you can keep your car here until we get back. But... you might not love it, what with the whole mortal enemies turned lovers kind of vibe we've got going on. This place is different."

"A challenge? You're on, Doctor Murphy. Lead the way."

This was going to either blow up in my face or turn into the best night of my life. Chances were pretty good for the former, but I was willing to take my chances on the latter.

CHAPTER SEVENTEEN

ASHLYN

"*A*re you ever going to tell me where we're going?" Rex asked for the thousandth time. I was having the time of my life holding this secret in. He was probably going to kill me when he found out where we were going, but he'd get over it. He was a pro at rolling with the punches. I just hoped literal punches didn't end up happening.

"No need. We're here." I pulled into the parking lot at Murphy's, the pub that my brother Brennan and his wife, Samantha, owned in Brandon Bay. He had the best seafood chowder in West Ireland and I so rarely took the hour drive to come see them, that I couldn't help but take Rex here for what I was calling our first official date. How we even went at the speed of light, I wasn't sure, but what could I do? The new Ashlyn was giving it a shot.

It was probably bad mojo to have your first official date at the restaurant your over-protective, big, alpha brother owned. But I needed someone other than Ox and Violet, two opposing opinions on Rex, to give me their opinion. I wasn't good at trusting my judgement and even though I would probably live to regret it, I wanted Sam and Brennan's blessing to continue exploring something with him. Of course, when the fact he was trying to buy the land our parents had left me got out, there would probably be no hope for him. But, I was confident I could get in and out before that became common knowledge.

It was also probably bad mojo to not tell your date that you were on your first official date. The Irish fairies were most likely dancing with glee at my insanity tonight.

"Murphy's Pub." Realization dawned and I could see the dots connecting by the expression on his face. "Oh shit. Ashlyn"—he turned in his seat to give me the stare down—"tell me you did not take me to eat at a restaurant owned by a family member tonight."

I smiled as best I could without turning it into a psycho-expression. "Guilty! But, Rex, seriously. You're going to love the food here. Best chowder around."

His face said he wasn't anywhere near being sold on the chowder. "Babe, you should have told me. I'm wearing a fucking suit. If anyone in there is related to you, they're going to take one look at me and turn me right back out the way I came in. This is not 'Pub and meet the family' Rex."

He was probably right. My brother's pub was on the edge of the bay, just outside of the tiny seaside town of Castlegregory. It served great food, but it was still a pub. No one went inside dressed like Rex unless someone had either died or had recently returned from court.

"Stop worrying. You look great. But maybe put that hair back. I'm not sure my brother could handle the suit and the hair at the same time."

"Your brother! Jesus Christ, Ashlyn. I take you on our first date and you bring us to your brother's place?"

"Our first date?" Well, at least we were on the same page.

"Focus, babe. This isn't gonna be good."

"It's not like it's his house. This is his restaurant. And my cousin Ryan works here too. And my sister-in-law Sam might be here with the kids. That'll soften the blow. I mean, if there is one, which of course, there will not be. Bren is—"

"Staring at us through the windows."

"He's wha—" Shit. He was right. Brennan was definitely staring at me. He raised an eyebrow and jerked his head to the left to signal me to get a move on. Brennan was an intimidating guy if you didn't know he was a complete softy. Tall, jet-black hair like mine, a full, neatly trimmed beard and always dressed in black.

"Okay, just follow my lead, got it?"

He let out a sigh and turned to face me. "Babe, it'll be fine. I've been in worse situations."

"That's lead number one. No 'babe.' Brennan will go nuts if he thinks I've been hiding something from him. Like the fact that you are a guy who currently calls me babe."

"Let's just get this over with." He opened the door to get out but I reached over and yanked him back in.

"Number two. The hair. Tie it back, kind of, I don't know, low profile-like." I flinched as I watched him question every single decision that had led him to come here with me tonight. "Sorry, sorry. Hair down. Leave it. Definitely, hair down."

He stared at me and my eyes bugged out when I figured out his next move was to kiss me senseless with my big brother attempting to annihilate me with his laser-eyes. "Rex, God. As much as I enjoy your kisses, this isn't helping our case."

He pulled back and narrowed his eyes. "We have a case?"

I tried to tame his hair as it was currently stuck to one of my eyelashes. "No, no case. Shit, let's just get this over with. Why I ever thought this would be a good idea is beyond me. It was looking like trying to be a different, more impulsive version of myself was such a bad idea.

"Leave your hair, leave your suit. We're doomed anyhow. He's crossed his arms. It's his tell. He's pissed and our only hope is if his wife or daughters are close by. Then, we're golden. He's only a dick to everyone on earth except when they're around."

He just shook his head, smoothed his hair back and got out, leaving me to my guilty conscience. I scrambled out after him, trying to get to the door first. No dice. He barged on in like he owned the place, just like he always did, and marched right up to Brennan.

By the time I had fully caught up, they were shaking hands and laughing. Thirty seconds. Thirty fucking seconds and I was already screwed over by Rex. Bros before ho's and all that bullshit. I was going to kill him. If only he wasn't a magic orgasm giver. That was a definite snag in the death plan. I did enjoy that orgasm and wanted a few more before he died.

"Ash," Bren said turning his full alpha-male, big brother personality on me, "why didn't you tell me you were bringing your new boyfriend here tonight?"

"Well, for starters, I didn't know he was my boyfriend?" I looked at Rex with one eyebrow raised.

Brennan turned back to the questionable boyfriend and slapped him on the shoulder while walking away. "Good luck with her, brother. She's always been the challenging one. Why someone decided to give me two belligerent sisters, I'll never know. I'll send someone over to take your order."

And he just walked away. Without even saying hi or giving me a hug. What in the ever-loving hell had just happened? I turned to face Rex when I saw Ryan coming at us. Ryan was our actual cousin, but in truth, was more like a brother. I needed him to come over to us like a hole in the head, so I dragged Rex towards an ocean facing booth with the hopes of getting a little privacy while I freaked out.

"What in the hell did you say to him?" I whisper yelled.

"Who? Brennan? I just complimented him on the place, told him you've been a pain in my side, but I wasn't about to let you go, and could I get a beer." A beer landed in front of him, with my standard Diet Pepsi and lime being placed in front of me by none other than the cousin-brother I didn't want to see right now.

"Thanks, Ry. Now, go away."

"Now, Ashlyn Murphy. Your mother would be appalled at your behavior. Introduce your friend here to me now and I'll be on my way."

I rolled my eyes and waved my hand in Rex's direction. "Rex, this is Ryan, my cousin and co-owner of this establishment. Ryan, this is my friend, Rex. Now get lost." I looked at Rex's shocked face and tried the kinder, gentler approach. "Please?"

He ignored me and slid in beside me. "You'll have to excuse our Ashlyn. She's always been a headstrong girl. Tell me, Rex, are you the very same Rexford McDaniel the Third who is looking to purchase the land that our Ashlyn currently owns?"

Rex smiled and attempted to charm a master charmer. Good luck with that buddy. "I am."

"The same Rex that our girls have said would be the perfect match for our Ashlyn here? The one with the long, flowing hair and the rear assets to die for?"

Now it was Rex's turn to throw his head back and roar with laughter. "I might be." He turned to me and winked. Winked! The cheeky bastard.

"Well now, if you are that Rex, then I wish you luck with this one, my friend. She's got a solid mind of her own and isn't afraid to use it. And the heart of a lamb, so don't fucking step on it. Now, what can I get you two to eat?"

And just like that the consummate charmer redeemed

himself and I knew I was getting tag teamed by Ryan and my brother playing good-cop, bad-cop. It appeared Ryan had drawn the short straw this time around.

He took our orders and left, finally, and I stared awkwardly at my date. "So..."

He lifted his glass and tapped it to mine. "Cheers, babe. Looks like we passed inspection and in record time. Now that that's out of the way, start talking. What else about you don't I know? Are we stopping at all your other relatives' houses along the way home?"

"I'm sorry. I was just, I don't know, happy. And I wanted to find somewhere that reminded me that I was safe. Even if you trampled all over my heart, I still had my family here. So, I drove to the only place that could do that for me. Brennan's pub."

He reached across and grabbed a hold of my hand and started slowly rubbing his thumb across it. "Ashlyn, stop. I can handle a couple of brothers. But if this thing with us is going to work, we're going to have to start to be honest and trust each other."

"You see, Rex, that's just it. I don't trust you."

CHAPTER EIGHTEEN

REX

*O*f course she didn't trust me. She shouldn't trust me. I had no fucking clue what I was playing at but it wouldn't be long before Daddy Dearest swooped in and ruined it all. I was off-script, that was for damn sure and I was in danger of losing this entire game. Miller, the dog and now, Ashlyn. The problem was, I wanted to keep them all. I wanted the white picket Irish fence with the beautiful woman, the crazy kid and her messed up dog. Something had snapped inside me and now I just had to figure out how to proceed. For now, I was here and I didn't plan on leaving without her. It wasn't often I got free time like this. I was going to milk every damn minute of it.

"You might not believe it, but I've had my fair share of big brother drama. And for the record, you can trust me." God, that guilty feeling was taking root inside my stomach.

She looked at me and I knew she wasn't buying it, but maybe we both could pretend for the night that the other didn't need something. I knew now I needed something, but it wasn't exclusively her land anymore.

Today in her office was unexpected. Hell, realizing that all

I wanted to do was to be close to her was unexpected. I was in. All I had to do was stall my father until I could come up with a viable alternative to pushing her off her land. And perform the simple act of making her fall for me in twenty-four hours so potentially, she'd stick with me through the mud. Nothin' to it.

"Fine. I'll let you stay," she said. "But if you side with my brother again, I'll murder you and you won't even know it. I've got ways. Understand? For years, my brothers all thought they could boss Keeva and me around and the last thing I need is someone who's supposed to be on my side joining their team."

"Your little sister, right?" I was desperately trying to remember which sister was which back from that murky night in the bar in Galway and her various throw away comments.

She smiled and I could tell the two were close. "Yes, my baby sister. Who will get a real kick when she hears about me being here with you. I wouldn't put it past her to be on her way here by now. I can guarantee Bren's called her, Aiden and Quinn already. This is what happens when you have a big family and they're Irish and live within driving distance. They converge. So, let's eat and see if we can escape before more of them come."

She had me pegged all wrong. I was the only child of a powerful asshole. I'd spent the majority of my childhood on my knees praying for siblings. And friends. Didn't have many of those either. Up until I met my ex, I didn't let myself get too close to many people. That typically led to absolutely nothing good. A large family sounded pretty damn awesome to me.

I swung my arms out wide and smiled, which I knew irritated her even more, which was fucking adorable. "Bring them on. I've got nowhere to be for a change." She chewed her bottom lip and I could tell she was completely off-balance and damn, it was fun.

"It's just you and Miller? No one else?"

I raised an eyebrow. This was an interesting development. "No one else, Ashlyn. You probably wouldn't believe me if I told you, but I'll do it anyway. Since I landed here last year, there's been only one person. And I believe you found something that belonged to her inside my dog. And at the risk of looking like a slob, that had been under my bed for quite some time.

"No one but my daughter. She's my world. She's my life and I'll do anything to keep her happy. So, no. No new people in her life since we moved here. Things haven't been easy for her and I owe it to her to shut down the revolving door of women I used to have."

Her eyes bugged out and I laughed.

"I had assumed you might have had a string of, well, you know." There she was, getting all adorable again.

"No, I don't know. What do you mean?"

"Stop. You know what I was trying to say. I just, well…" She fidgeted with the napkin and stared at a spot off in the distance. She finally turned and appeared to have worked up the nerve to look me in the eye. "Look, you're hot. That hair, those muscles, your suit habit and the daughter and the dog? Please. Women don't stand a chance resisting you. Seriously."

"Okay, and so?"

"And so…" she was back to fooling with the napkin, "…it's just logical that I thought you might have someone."

And now I was pissed. Not because she thought that, but that because she thought I would do that to her. "Babe." She swung her head back to me. "I'm gonna say this once and then I don't want to have to repeat myself. Got it?"

She nodded.

"The plan wasn't to want you. Tonight, I didn't know

what the hell I was doing, but I was frustrated with work and just blindly got in my car and drove to you. Only you. I don't fuck around. I wouldn't bring anyone into my life who I didn't think understood that. Miller changed me. You didn't know me before, but know that she changed me for the better. You? You were a sneak attack, but I'm in. Two extra-large feet, all the way in."

I paused, wiggling my eyebrows making her softly laugh as intended. "There's going to be things that we'll need to get past and they won't always be easy. But I'm not sitting here, thinking about finishing what we started tonight and then moving on. I'm sitting here wondering how in the hell I'm going to juggle two obstinate females and a hyper dog. I'm sitting here wondering why I waited so long to make a move and I'm also sitting here telling you there are some ladies who must be related to you staring us down."

She whipped her head around and groaned. "Damn," she whispered. "Do not make eye contact. The tall blonde?"

"Samantha Lane. Recognize her from a mile away."

"Yes, well, that's Brennan's wife."

"Shit. Well, there goes that fantasy," I joked.

"Very funny." She slapped my arm and narrowed her eyes at me. "The little one beside her is Chloe. That's Ryan's wife. And the tiny shit disturber, you—"

I got up and wrapped Keeva Murphy in a hug, air kissing her cheek. "Keeva Murphy. Great to see you again."

"Wow, record time, Keev. You beat Quinn and Vi. But only because they would have had to bundle up the twins before they raced you here. Where's Nix?"

"Shove over, Lynny," Keeva tried to muscle her way into the booth. Samantha and Chloe had chosen to stay over by the bar and observe. This evening had just gotten a hell of a lot more entertaining. I had a front row seat to the childhood I had always wanted.

"Get lost Keeva. I hate to break it to you, but you drove all the way down here for nothing. Rex and I were just leaving and remind me to bash Bren's head in on the way by."

"No one's bloody well bashing my fucking head in. Keeva"—Brennan nodded his head towards the bar—"go keep Sam and Chloe company. Give her a little space for fuck's sakes. They just got here."

Keeva stuck out her tongue at Ashlyn, who promptly rolled her eyes and then flashed them at Brennan. "Thanks, Bren," she said.

"Don't thank me. I've only held them off. They'll be over here once you're done eating. My advice? Eat slow." He burst out laughing, having amused himself and turned and left.

Ashlyn looked at me, her eyes flashing fury and I was stuck. I could either reach out and quietly brush the stray hairs away from her eyes, trying to sooth her. Or I could grab her hand again and gently stroke her palm. Or I could just smile and sit back and enjoy the show. All three options would irritate her and amuse me.

Fuck it. I reached across and swept the crazy lock of hair that refused to be tamed off her face, tucking it behind her ear. "This is the most fun I've had since Mills made me dress up as Kristoff and then made me try to ride one of the horses around her pretend version of Arrandale. Please, don't worry about me. Let them come and let them try to figure us out. It'll be fun."

"Oh God. Now you've done it," she said.

I looked up as I was shoving fries into my mouth and saw Ashlyn staring and smiling and I couldn't help but smile back. "What?"

"You gonna make out with that fry? You've got a little drool there, buddy." Like I said. Adorable. She was finally relaxing. If I had my way, she'd be as relaxed as she'll ever be in a few hours.

"What! Where? Can you get it?"

"Smooth move, Exlax."

"Do people even say that anymore? What are you? Five?" God I was having fun. I didn't want this to end, but it would and then I had no clue what I'd do. I still had the rather large problem of my father and her land to figure out.

"Rex. You okay?" she asked.

"Yup, just sad that these fries will soon be gone to a better place. Come on, eat up. They look like they're dying over there. Let's get through this so we can get on to the good stuff." I popped another fry into my mouth, held back a groan and dug into my fish. This would have to be cheat day this week. The only thing I had for myself was working out. Miller knew if Dad was in the gym that I had built in our outbuilding, only near death was allowed to interrupt me.

"The good stuff?"

She'd stopped chewing and her face had gone pale. The little minx was scared. Good, let her sweat a bit. I liked a challenge. I just smiled at her and continued eating making her jump to her own conclusions.

"Come on, babe. Eat up. You'll need your strength." Shit, this was too easy. She rubbed her forehead and was squirming in her seat. *That's right sweetheart. I'm going to fucking rock your world. Get ready.*

She threw a French fry at my head and I caught it with my mouth, just to prove to her I meant business. Circus business maybe, but still, I was ready for whatever she had to throw at me tonight.

"Stop, Rex. You're just feeding their fire." She puckered up her mouth and tried to look angry but failed miserably. "What do you say we get them over here so they can have their fun and get out of here?"

"Preaching to the choir, babe."

She signaled to her family to come over and I battened

down the hatches for what would surely rival the Spanish Inquisition. Sisters and sisters-in-law were no joke. "Ladies."

Their spokeswoman was first to volley. Samantha Lane was both an international superstar and the girl next door. Beautiful but approachable and from what I'd briefly seen, hell on wheels. "Rex. Slide over."

I did as I was told and reached under the table to brush Ashlyn's knee with my hand. She looked miserable, poor thing. "Ouch." I turned to find Samantha pinching my arm and looking for God knows what. "What did you do that for?"

"Zero body fat. That's never good," she said.

"What? Why the hell not?"

"Also, swearing in a public place." She smiled and I let out the breath I'd been holding in. If I was being honest, being shoulder to shoulder with a superstar like her was giving me a mild case of the hives. I could see why Ashlyn was so nervous to have them come over. Alone, they were fine, but together, they were out for blood.

"Sam, leave him alone," Ashlyn said.

Sam turned to focus her attention on Ashlyn and I felt minimally better. But only for a brief second. "Have you slept with him?" she asked. That was more than I had bargained for.

Ashlyn rolled her eyes and leaned over the table. "Samantha Lane, how did you like it when my brother broadcasted your love life to this very pub each and every night?"

Sam narrowed her eyes on her sister-in-law and their silent war reached what appeared to be a stalemate.

"So? Have you?" This from Keeva. The baby of the family and the one I was the least terrified of. From what I could gather, I was still missing out on half the family. I needed to reassess before getting into the car with Ashlyn anymore.

"Keeva!" Ashlyn whisper yelled. "Get a hold of yourself. We are not discussing this here."

"Aha!" exclaimed Keeva. "Here. Which means we will be discussing it somewhere at some point in time." She stole a fry off her sister's plate. "I can live with that." She chewed and grabbed another fry, this time using it as a pointer, directing it right at my face. "So, Mr. Fancy Pants, why are you two here?"

"I'm not exactly sure." I looked at the third guest who up to this point, had sat there silently observing. "Rexford McDaniel. And you are?"

I held out my hand for Chloe to take. Her eyes bulged and she looked to the ringleader for her next step. Samantha turned to fully face me and I braced for impact. "Okay, Mr. Rexford McFancypants, stay away from the shy one. Chloe isn't wired for the likes of you. So, you won't tell us if you've done the deed, but will you tell us what your intentions are?"

Oh, this was going to be extra, extra fun. I ran a hand through my hair and prepared for Ashlyn's fury. "I intend to take her back to my place or hers and see where things go from there. I intend to have her in every way imaginable and I intend to prove to her that she can trust me. Right now, she's ready to murder me, but would I be correct in the assumption that you will not let us leave until you know exactly who I am and what I am going to do with your sister tonight?"

"You would be."

"So, ladies, let's just cut to the chase."

"Rex—"

I grabbed a hold of Ashlyn's hand and gave it a reassuring squeeze. "Babe, it's okay. I'll answer her questions."

I turned back to find all three of them gaping at me. "What?"

Sam was the first to find her footing. "You called her Babe."

"Yes, and?"

"And she didn't slap you." This from Keeva.

"No." I smiled. "She didn't the first time I called her that either. She was actually rather bus—"

Ashlyn dug her nails into my hand and I received the message loud and clear. I didn't have any sibling experience. I'd need her killer nail signals to guide me.

"Next question."

"Are you her boyfriend?" Chloe asked.

"Well, if she'll have me I am. But I'm afraid we haven't gotten that far yet. I assumed, incorrectly, for the longest time that she rather hated me."

"You weren't incorrect." Ashlyn looked at me with a definite hint of anger. That paired with her sharpening nails and I guess we were nearly at departure time. I hadn't had this much fun with a woman, well, ever. Miller's mother was an ice queen who I made the mistake of assuming loved me for me, and not the millions my father was considering leaving me, and prior to her, I wasn't much for long term anything.

"You were right to not trust me, Ashlyn. I still don't really know where this is going, so if you want to back out of tonight, now's the time."

The booth fell silent and I realized I'd temporarily forgotten about our audience. Ashlyn looked at her sisters and somehow communicated through girl code that it was time for them to go. They all silently got up and hugged Ashlyn goodbye and took off to their respective partners.

Ashlyn sat back down and grabbed my hands. "Well, this took a turn into downer town, didn't it? Rex? I really never hated you. I hope you know that. Wanted you to fuck off a time or two? Yup. That was for damn sure."

I laughed and looked out at the churning ocean that came

up alongside the pub's parking lot. There were a few kids playing at the nearby playground and I briefly wondered if Miller was okay. I hadn't been away from her all that much since I'd taken sole custody for this long. I was itching to check in on her even though Maisie forbade me to.

"Those are Brennan's kids," Ashlyn whispered. "The big one is Claire. She's his from a previous disastrous relationship. Her mother gave up custody to Brennan when Claire was 6 months old. You two have a lot in common. The wild boy is Max, and the blonde with the curls is Fiona, their daughter. You should bring Miller here one day. She'd love that bunch. Add in Chloe and Ryan's daughter and the four amigos will show her the ropes of growing up Irish-American. I can't guarantee she won't get in trouble, of course, but they are good kids."

"She would love that. Thanks."

She grabbed my hand and tugged me out of the booth. "Come on. Let's get out of here. I want to show you something."

I dug in my pocket to pay, but found a large hand clamping down on my shoulder. "Don't bother," Brennan said. "Family doesn't pay here."

The guilt moved up a notch and I began again to question this path I had chosen. She had family. My family wanted to hurt her family. But what I'd felt over the fast few hours with her was offering me a piece of something I'd never had. A real family.

"Thanks, man." Ashlyn tugged on my hand but Brennan had yet to let go.

"Bren! Let him go," Ashlyn whispered.

Brennan smiled and I was reminded of a wolf. The man didn't fuck around, that was for sure. "Lynny, this will just take a second. He'll be with you in a minute."

Ah, and here was the big brother talk I'd been waiting for.

Shit, this first date was going to go down in the record books. "It's okay, Ashlyn. Go say goodbye. I'm fine."

"Well, duh. Of course you're fine. Just don't say anything to make Bren cry." She walked away laughing to herself and I fell just a little bit harder.

"You've got it bad."

I shrugged. Whatever he thought it was I had, I wasn't sure I wanted it. Miller was first in my world. There wasn't room for anyone else. This was so new and I was still trying to sort it all out. What I did have bad was a basic need for that woman who was now waiting for me to take her home to her bed.

"I know what you're thinking. She told me a bit about you here and there. I raised Claire on my own with a dirtbag for an ex. I don't know your story, but I do know what it feels like to want to protect your family. Ash is tough. She doesn't do much else other than work and protect our family. She's not going to move in and push your daughter out of the picture. And yes, there is room for someone else and it won't hurt what you have."

I eyed him up and wondered if mind reading was another one of his powers. He'd hit a nerve, but I was pretty sure my social climbing ex could take his on. I crossed my arms and stared out the picture windows to the kids playing by the ocean across the street. "I don't know. There's other stuff at play. Miller's mom is a fucking piece of work. She only wants the money that comes with her and my dad uses that against me."

Shit, where had that come from? I'd never told another soul. I hadn't even thought I'd tell Ashlyn.

"Ah. The land? You're chasing her for the land?" His voice had become strained and I was in a serious danger zone.

"I'm not chasing her for anything she has other than herself." I uncrossed my arms and put my hands in my pockets so they didn't give anything away. "But my father thinks with his bank account and I have to do what's best for my daughter first, me second. So, yeah, I don't really know where that leaves us."

He turned to stand beside me and face the kids as well. "You have to tell her where you're at at all times. You can't string her along and then take it all away. She'll never recover."

"I know."

Someone called his name and he gave me one last look that if I was any other guy, would have me running the other way. But I grew up a McDaniel. There wasn't much in the intimidation arena I hadn't adapted to. I could handle her brother.

"Don't fuck this up." And with those wise parting words, he left to attend to whatever it was he was needed for. I stood for one more second, watching the kids run and scream and knew I had to see this through. It was time to break the pattern. Miller needed other kids, other people. People she could rely on. Family. And I needed Ashlyn Murphy.

CHAPTER NINETEEN

ASHLYN

"Come on. We're almost there. Open your eyes, you big baby."

Rex had shut his eyes at the first sign of the single lane that climbed to the top of the hill. Something had gotten to him during dinner and there wasn't much an Irish sunset couldn't pull out of someone. I was determined to figure this man out. He'd gone from hot to cold to asshole and back to hot so fast I had severe whiplash.

"Just one more hairpin turn. You're missing the best parts."

He cracked open one eye and I giggled. "Laugh one more time and I'll show you just how manly I really am right out here in the open. This is just a bump in my manly road. Lots of manly men are afraid of driving in Ireland."

I pursed my lips and pretended to close my eyes. "Shit, Ashlyn. Get two hands on that wheel. Ten and two. Ten and fucking two."

It was too easy. He truly was afraid. Too bad we were just about there. It would have been fun stretching this out a bit longer. Going down on the other side was a piece of cake. I pulled into the car park and turned to face him. I gently pried his hands off his face. "Open your eyes and check out my favourite spot on earth."

He did as I told him to and I watched him see what this country could offer. From up on this cliff, the setting sun felt like you could just reach out and touch it. It was slowly sinking into the ocean in a swirling mass of pastels and I sighed. "Come on," I opened my car door. "It's even better when you're sitting on the edge."

He nervously followed me across the street and I was happy to see we were the only ones here. I sat down on the edge of the earth and patted the spot beside me. "Come on. Grab a seat. The show won't last for much longer."

He hesitated. "Are you sure this is safe?"

"Get down here. Your manhood is once again in question." I pulled him down beside me. "So, why's your hair long?"

He looked nervous but was trying, I'd give him points for that. We were sitting on the edge of a cliff. There was a grassy outcrop below us, but not much else to break our fall. "It pissed off my dad at first. Then I just got comfortable with it and now? Now I'm not sure I know how to be me without it."

"Hm."

He nudged me cautiously with his shoulder. "Hm? What's that mean?"

"It just means, hm. Makes sense, but…"

"But?"

"But I think you use it to hide who you really are from everyone who meets you. And, yes, to also probably piss off your father."

"When'd you get your psych degree?"

I laughed and scooted back from the edge, flopping down on my back, staring up at the darkening sky. "We should probably get going. It's an hour back to my house and then you'll still have to drive home."

He flopped down beside me and turned his head to look into my eyes. "Who said I'm going home tonight?"

He rolled into me while sliding his hand underneath my neck and holding me still with his other hand across my waist. He softly landed a kiss across my mouth, once, twice, then his tongue slid out, seeking entry.

I wiggled away from the edge of the cliff and rolled up against him, flattening my body to his, resting my hand against his chest, where I could feel the solid beating of his heart. "Rex, I don't know what we're doing here."

"Me neither. Why aren't we somewhere where there's a bed?" he said as he rained kisses across my face and neck. "And a roof over our heads and immanent death not nearby."

I sighed. I shouldn't trust him. I barely knew him and what I knew was full of turmoil and anger. But this man who I'd spent the past few hours with was a complete juxtaposition from the man I thought he was. This man was strong, kind, brave and still sexy as hell. Regardless of how I felt about him, he'd always been hot. I was an ass girl and Rexford McDaniel the Third had an ass for the record books.

I broke free and dropped a kiss on his nose. "Okay, let's go to my place then."

He smiled. "Your place it is."

He slowly got up and I had to wonder if he'd ever been to a cliff in Ireland. The whole damn country was a stone's throw from a cliff. And the cliffs here didn't have much in the way of safety rails. A stiff wind was incredibly dangerous to anyone who ventured near.

He held out a hand and helped pull me up. I snapped a quick selfie of us and the sunset much to his chagrin and got us on our way. The drive home was quiet, both of us lost in our thoughts.

For my part, I spent the hour alternating between imagining him naked in my bed and him betraying me by somehow tricking me into giving him my land. But by the time we had arrived back at my place, the naked vision had fully taken over and I'd gotten myself so worked up, I could hardly stop myself from jumping across the front seat and making out like a love-sick teenager.

He must have been thinking along the same lines because as soon as we parked and got inside the door, he pushed me against the wall and began urgently divesting me of all of my clothes. I kindly returned the favour and we spent the next few minutes wrestling each other out of their clothes.

Naked, I stood and admired my handywork. He raised a single eyebrow and smirked like he thought he was all that and a slice of toast. Of course, he was fucking right, but if I wanted my brother and his girlfriend to admire him right along with me, I needed to move our operation up to my bedroom and away from my front door.

I lived in a barn conversion that was open living at its finest. My rooms were upstairs in the loft area and unfortunately, there was a lot of glass between our current location and my room.

I looked at Rex and smiled. "Ready to run, Rexford?"

"You're on, Princess."

I took off, using the advantage of the knowledge of where I was going and my long legs to get a jump on him. Once we hit the stairs, he gained on me. I was out of breath, laughing and squealing like a little girl by the time he easily caught me around the waist just before I'd made it to the safety of my oversized king bed. I'd never had a guest in my bed, but being a tall girl, I always liked having the room to stretch out.

"Got you," he whispered seductively in my ear, sending shivers up and down my back. Nuzzling my neck from behind, his hands began exploring my body while he kept my brain occupied with his talented lips and tongue.

I wasn't in love with my body. I was tall. I had curves and I certainly wasn't ever described as tiny, but somehow, his hands, his lips and his insistent cock pushing into my back made me feel like the most beautiful woman in the world.

He turned me around in his arms and our mouths found each other, tongues fighting for power, hands drawn like magnets to each other's ass, squeezing, massaging and frantically trying to gain some ground against the swell that was threatening to overtake us.

We came apart and he just stood there, staring at me. "Hi," he whispered.

"Hi."

"Are you sure, Ashlyn? We can—"

I fell backwards, taking him with me, making sure to leave no doubt about how much I wanted him inside me that very moment.

He stretched out over top of my body, still looking at me with wonder. "Mmm, you're very persuasive when you want to be, Doctor Murphy."

"No more talking."

"Roger that."

He bent his head, slowly tasting me across my chest until he got to my breasts. Taking one in hand and the other in his mouth, he circled my nipple, effectively driving my hips up and off the bed with a pleasure that was ricocheting around inside my core. "Mm, that worked well."

I grabbed his ass and pinched as hard as I could to signal my displeasure at his chatting. He answered with a forceful tug on my nipple making me squeak in mock protest. He promptly moved to the other breast, giving it the same amount of attention while I squirmed underneath him, trying to telepathically make him understand what I needed.

"Greedy girl. I've pictured this for too long to rush this, babe. Be still. I want to know every inch of you before this night is over."

Shit, did he not realize I had been in a monogamous relationship for the past few years with my vibrator. The time for patience was long gone. Frustrated, I flipped us over and pinned him to the bed with my hands over his impressive biceps.

"Time's up. Quick first, slow second."

He got the message that playtime was over. I reached past him to my side table, opening it and pulling out my stash of wishful thinking condoms that had finally paid off. Every year I replenished the box with new condoms thinking that maybe that year was going to be my year. The problem was, workaholics didn't leave much time for bedroom action. I held the strip up in front of his face with what I hoped was a smug look on my face.

He flipped us again so I was back on the bottom. "I love a prepared woman. Good thing you've got so many, since you're such a demanding woman."

"Less talking, and more getting on with it."

He smiled and got down to the business of putting on the condom. I opened my legs, reaching for him to pull him into me, slowly, deliciously.

He started moving, filling me up, seeking, churning, making me ache with need and feelings of pure pleasure. Whatever happened between the two of us from this point on was irrelevant. Right here, right now? This was the stuff of my romance novels. Classic enemies to lovers, frantically trying to erase all the anger that had preceded this moment in time and use that pent-up frustration with each other for good and not evil.

He picked up the pace, leaving slow and leisurely behind, in exchange for frenzied and demanding, until finally, with the flick of his finger on my clit, he sent me over the edge, where he followed only moments later.

Slowing, we came down together, kissing like it was all we ever did. A new level of comfort with each other. "Baby."

There it was again. That term of endearment I never thought I wanted, but apparently had just been hearing it from the wrong men. "Yes?"

He didn't say anything, just dropped a simple, sweet kiss on my lips, then fell down beside me in all his naked glory. I rolled over to get a good look at him, propped up on one elbow, head resting in my hand.

"Why have we spent all of our time arguing and none of our time doing that?" he asked me.

"Good question. Should we go again to see if that time was a fluke?"

"Give an old man a minute, babe."

"Sure thing, captain. I'll just lie here and admire the view." I traced a finger over his impossibly hard and sculpted chest, down the ridges of his abs, stopping short of his impressive hard-on.

"Let me take care of the condom and then we'll talk." He headed for the bathroom I'd indicated and disposed of the condom, allowing me a moment to let the doubt come creeping back in. "Oh no you don't," he crawled back in bed, pinning me underneath him again. "I can see it written all over your face. Stop whatever you're thinking again and just be here with me now."

He rolled off me and took his turn lying on his side, head propped up in his hand, and stared at me. My nipples, the little hussies, enjoyed his undivided attention, standing up, showing off and begging to be touched again.

He reached out a finger, tracing around them, making them dance to the music only he and they could hear. I tried to grab his hand away, but he gave me his patented threatening look and that, in combination with his wild hair, and impressive chest and arm muscles, made me decide to let him have his fun.

His roving finger slowly descended past my belly button and on to previously enjoyed adventures, stopping to drive me back up the flag pole of pleasure, when it landed on my clit, slowly, delicately driving me insane.

"Rex," I breathed out. "Please."

"Please what, baby?"

"More. Please."

He was still, with the exception of his skilled hand, while I was struggling to stay on the bed. His hand spread my legs open, leaving me exposed and open for whatever he had in mind.

He dragged his finger up my opening, stopped ever so slightly to tease me and then carried on, heading back up towards my belly button.

"Rex?"

"Yes?"

"Do not tease me."

"Wouldn't dream of it, darling." He paused to grab another condom from my supply, quickly putting it on and plunging inside me all in the manner of a few breaths. I arched up and off the bed, exhaling as he slowly tortured me from the inside out. "Better?"

"Yes, very much so."

"We aim," he punctuated with a particularly powerful thrust, "to please."

We spent most of the night trading places of power, mirroring our relationship up to that point outside of the bedroom. The big difference being inside my bed, I was more than willing to give up control to him. I wasn't sure what the morning light would bring, but I forgot to care after orgasm numbers three and four.

CHAPTER TWENTY

ASHLYN

I woke the next morning to someone in my house frantically yelling my name. "Ash! Yo, Ash?" Shit, shit, shit. It was Ox.

I quickly threw my exhausted body out of bed and grabbed the first piece of clothing I could find, which happened to be Rex's gorgeous tailored white dress shirt. Quickly buttoning it up, I was only focused on one thing. Making sure Ox did not come up to the loft level.

"Ox! What in the hell are you doing inside my house?" I rushed out to the landing that overlooked the main floor and came to a frozen halt. Too late, I realized that I was dressed only in a man's shirt and nothing else and I was tall. I wasn't leaving much to the imagination. It didn't matter whose shirt, but to Ox, it would be pretty obvious someone was still in my bed. Of course, my wild hair and lack of undergarments would also be a dead giveaway.

"Jesus Christ, Ash. Put some fucking clothes on and get to the barns. Maggie's about to foal."

"You might want to talk to her with a little more respect."

And fuck my life. That voice that coaxed my orgasms out

all night long, was now next levelling the tension in my house.

"Him? Ash? What the fuck have you done?"

"None of your Goddamned business, Ox. I'll be in the barn in ten."

He just stood there, alternating shooting daggers between Rex and me. Strong arms wrapped around me from behind and I leaned back, feeling torn between one of my best friends and the man I was falling for. Ox had no right barging in here and judging me. He could have used the phone like most normal people to wake me up.

He abruptly turned on his heel and shot back down the stairs, marching back the way he had come and I swung around, resting my head on the steel chest behind me.

"You okay?"

I sighed. "Yes, I'll be fine. But I better get to work. I'm sorry." I looked up into his eyes and really, really could have killed Maggie for doing this to me right now. "Stay as long as you need to. Towels are in the closet in the bathroom. There's food in the fridge. I'll just need to grab some clothes, brush my teeth and head to the barns."

He bent down and lightly kissed my lips. "I'm good. I've got to go get Miller anyway."

I kissed him back and dove into my drawer full of clean jeans, hastily pulling them on and a shirt over my head.

"I was thinking," he said.

"Yes?" I had clothes on and was brushing my hair, pulling it back and tying it off for the day.

"Maybe you could come over for dinner tonight?"

I smiled to myself. He was all sorts of adorable. "Love to. Just depends on how Maggie makes out. You could bring Miller here in the next little bit? As long as the birth goes well, she'll be able to see the baby."

I started brushing my teeth, focusing on trying to bring

some sense of order to my appearance when he stalked over to me in the bathroom and lifted me up onto the counter.

"Rex!" I spit out the toothpaste. "I have to get moving."

His mouth invaded mine. There was no other term for it. My legs instantly spread to give him better access, arms flying around him and legs wrapping him up like a present. I could feel his dick getting hard and knew that I had to cut this off before I missed the foaling.

"As much as this pains me to do so, I have to go. Raincheck?"

"Thank you."

He was looking at me so intently that it gave me a momentary pause. "For what?"

He rested his forehead against mine and held both sides of my face in his massive hands. "For not freaking out. For taking me to meet your family. For thinking of Miller just now before yourself. Fuck, this is pretty new to me, but I kind of like it."

I kissed him hard, directly on the lips. "If you only knew how long it had been for me, you might not be all that impressed. I'm a desperate woman, Rexford McDaniel. Desperate times, call for desperate measures."

He laughed and launched me into his arms, wedding style, carrying me back into my bedroom. Setting me down on the floor, he turned me towards the door, smacked me gently on the ass and shoved me forward. "Get going, Doctor Murphy. Before I take advantage of that sexual desperation that's written all over your face."

I laughed all the way down the stairs and across my yard to the barns. I entered the birthing area with what must have the goofiest grin on my face for seven in the morning on a Saturday.

"Okay, guys. How's she doing?" I started scrubbing my hands, studiously ignoring Ox's insistent glares in my direction. The last thing I needed was to deal with his moody ass this morning.

"She's nearly there, Doctor Murphy," Cameron, my vet tech said. "Perfect timing."

I finished scrubbing up, dried off my arms and hands and pulled on gloves I'd need on to help Maggie should she need it. I walked around her, checking her vitals and making sure she wasn't in any state of distress.

"She's all clear. We're good to go, Cam. Ox? You ready?"

He looked at me, raised an eyebrow and snapped on his gloves. Oh, he was going to play it like that then?

I walked out of the stall where the horse lay, to settle myself in for what should be a routine delivery. Maggie wasn't a first time mom, so things should go pretty smoothly.

I whispered words of encouragement through the open doorway to her stall to one of my favourite horses. A birth was always exciting, but with Maggie, my first horse at this farm, it was extra-special.

"Interesting." Ox came over and sat down on a stool beside me.

"What's interesting Ox?" I was tired, and deliciously sore and so not in the mood for his theatrics.

"Never pegged you for the type to sleep with just anyone who offered."

Oh he did not just throw that down in front of my employee. "Cam?"

"Just leaving, Doctor. I've got a few things to do in the clinic."

"Thank you, Cam. I'll come find you later once we're through."

He scrambled out the door, practically running for the safety of the next building, no doubt eager to let everyone know about Ox's statement.

I closed my eyes and rested my head against the stall wall.

"My love life is not your business and if you ever pull a stunt like that again, you will regret it."

"What were you thinking, Ash? You know he's using you."

His voice, coming from the other side of my eyeballs, sounded strained. The last thing I needed was for Violet to be right. Her assessment that he was in love with me was laughable. At least up until this moment I thought it was. Now, it sounded like he was more hurt than anything. And that most likely meant she was right.

"How do you know what he's doing?"

"I'm a man. I know his type."

Maggie shuddered, let out a cry and started moving around her stall on her side. It was almost time. We should be seeing something pretty soon.

"Yeah?" My eyes were still closed. I'd mastered the art of dozing during vet college. "And what type is that?"

"He'll sleep with you to get you to do what he needs you to do. He'll give you orgasms and you'll give him this land. Happily hand it over in exchange for his dick."

I opened my eyes, turned to face him and slapped him hard across his face. "When we're through here, I don't want to see you again for a good, long time. Say shit like that again and we're through permanently. Do you understand Ox?"

He pinched his face and fought to quell his anger. "I won't pick you up when he drops you like a stone when you sign the papers, so don't come crying to me, Ash."

I glared at him, clenching my fists and sucking in air. I wasn't going to stoop to his level and dignify his statement with a response. He stomped away and I got up and went into the stall to check on Mags. As I was standing there fuming, a tiny leg shot out of Maggie. "Yes. That's it girl. You know what to do now. Not long now my love."

She whinnied her reply and I backed up against the wall to give her the room she'd need to move around and push. It didn't matter if you were human, dog or horse, or whatever, the birthing process required room to move and now that she had a leg sticking out of her, she'd need all the help she could get.

I stood entranced, watching her labour and found myself thinking about childbirth as I often did in these situations. Poor, childless Ashlyn Murphy. My siblings were always asking me if I was ever going to find someone to procreate with. I was getting sick and tired of rolling my eyes and ignoring their question.

The hard truth was I desperately wanted to be a parent, but I was in no way interested in just getting pregnant for the sake of having a baby. I firmly wanted a partner for that life-long project. Up until this point, there had been zero contenders. There was no way I was heading in that direction with Rex. One incredible night of sex did not a lifelong partner make. That was a lesson I'd learned quickly in college.

Maggie hopped up, spun around and then flopped back down. This went on for a full thirty minutes and I was beginning to get ready to help things along. I checked my watch one final time and decided I needed to find Cam to come help me get the foal out. Maggie didn't need an extra leg sticking out of her privates any longer.

Since I'd banished Ox, I'd need Cam to help. It was typically a two-person job. One to calm the horse and one to reach in and get things to progress.

"Cam?" I called out. He wasn't supposed to be too far away.

"Can we help?" I whipped around at the sound of that voice. The one that had spent the night whispering dirty words in my ears.

"Yeah! We can totally help."

"Miller! Hey! Wow, you're here already. Have you ever

seen a foaling?" She was standing there, holding her dad's hand, blond hair pulled back in a messy pony tail, wearing the most unique mix and match outfit that only a child could pull off. Her eyes were as round as saucers and she had a look on her face that was a mix of horror and excitement. Her dad's face, funny enough, had the same look on it.

"No," she whispered. "I've never seen anything being born. Is it gross?"

"Well," I said. "That depends on your definition of gross. You see," I walked over to Maggie and pointed to the little leg sticking out of her. "This little leg belongs to her baby. But right now, that baby seems to be stuck and it just needs a little help from me to turn it around and then pop out. Now, when it pops out, yup, there's gross stuff that comes with it. But you forget about the gross stuff pretty quickly because suddenly, there's this adorable, beautiful miracle laying there that needs me and its mommy to take care of it."

"Hmm. Kind of like when I came out of my mom? Was I gross too?"

Rex was staring at her, looking like he was in another world. I still didn't know much about his past with Miller's mom but I supposed that would come later.

"You were so not gross, I am quite sure." I looked up at her dad and caught his eye and smiled. Now he was looking at me strangely, like he was on the verge of saying something, but holding back.

I skimmed his body and noticed for the first time that he was dressed casually. Loose jeans that hugged his ass and a T-shirt, worn and grey. He looked sexier than he did in his tailored suits, if that was even possible.

Of course, the signature mane was tied down and back off his neck in a high, sloppy man-bun. If I had the time, I'd seriously take a moment to examine the fact I was involved with a man who wore a man-bun. The one attribute I'd adamantly sworn I'd never be into. But there was no time for self-reflection right now. I had a foal to help along.

"What do you need us to do?" His question broke my reverie and just in time. Maggie was getting restless and we were out of time to see if she could bring this foal into the world on her own.

"Miller? You can be my timer, okay?" I gave her my phone which had the timer engaged. I set it at twenty minutes and started it. "Okay, every time a minute disappears, shout it out, okay?"

"Got it, Doctor Murphy."

"Great." I turned to Rex. "You'll want to put some gloves on. There should be a pair in a box beside you there. Then get in here. I need your muscles."

"Of course you do."

I rolled my eyes so hard I could see behind me. "Just get in here. Stop delaying your help. Wait." I stood up as I was moving Maggie into position. "Is this like your fear of driving on Irish roads? Are you squeamish too? God, McDaniel. Your reputation is in serious jeopardy this week."

He snapped on the gloves and marched into the stall. "My manliness is not in question here. Surely you, of all people, can attest to that."

I blushed and turned back to the horse. "Okay, I'm going to go in and try to move this little beast along. I need you to come around to the other side and keep Maggie from moving around too much. Miller?"

"Yes, Doctor?"

I smiled. The kid was adorable, just like her irritating, fraidy-cat of a dad. "Time left?"

"Seventeen minutes."

"Perfect. Thanks. Okay, I'm going in."

I gently eased my hand in ever so slightly, feeling around

for the sack that the foal would be wrapped in. Latching on, I began to pull it through the birth canal, slowly easing it out.

"You gonna pass out on me, McDaniel?"

He was desperately looking anywhere but at where my hands where. "I'm fine. Let's just get this over with."

"Fifteen minutes, Doctor Murphy," Miller yelled.

"Perfect. Thanks Miller. She's doing great."

Maggie moved a bit, hopped up and Rex and I both backed away, giving her the room to move around and to push her foal out. Ever so slowly, the sac emerged and we got our first glimpse of the foal. Maggie flopped back down, exhausted and ready to be done with this shit, I imagined.

"Rex?"

"Yup, right here. Being very manly."

I laughed and went in to give it one more pull. "Are you ready to catch the foal?"

The look on his face was all I needed to know. "Miller? Do you want to catch the foal?"

"But what about the timer?" she asked.

"We're good for time now. Now we just need to finish this so the mommy can start to care for her baby. And, since your daddy is a sissy pants, I'm going to need someone to help me who won't pass out at the sight of blood. Is that someone you?"

She set the phone down, grabbed a pair of gloves and snapped them on. "Yes, Doctor. I'm ready. Put me in!"

I threw my head back and laughed again. I couldn't remember the last time I'd had this much fun at work. "Well, get in here then. You're about to catch your first baby."

I guided her little hands over to where the sac was bulging out and ready to drop. With a gentle tug, the foal fully came out and Miller and I broke its fall to the ground. "Okay, here's the gross part."

"It hasn't been disgusting up until this point? Please," Rex said.

"Dad. Zip it."

"Yeah, zip it."

"Okay, now we need to tear the sac away for Maggie and get the little one clear. Ready?"

We tore the sac off the baby and I was able to quickly assess the health while Momma recovered enough to be able to care for the foal. "We don't want to touch the baby too much. Momma will want to scent…" I quickly lifted the foal's leg, "…her. It's a girl, Miller! Can you believe you just birthed a baby horse? You did so good."

We scooted the foal up closer to Maggie and sat back in the hay to watch the miracle that was the first time a mother and child are united. Maggie started to clean her baby in between rest periods.

I looked at my tiny assistant. "Well, Miller. Our job here is done for now. Let's go wash up."

Rex followed us out of the stall where I closed Maggie's gate and threw my gloves in the garbage. "Feeling better there, champ?"

"Ha, ha." He was still looking a little pale and a bead of sweat dripped down his temple.

"Dad! Did you see that? Oh my gosh! No one at school is ever going to top this. I can't wait for circle time. Pretty sure no one ever came back from home and shared that they birthed a horse!"

Miller went to lean on the gate to the stall and stare and Maggie and her new baby, enraptured with what she had just witnessed.

"Hey Miller?" I called to her.

"Yeah?"

"You've got another really important job, if you're up for it?"

167

Her face lit up. "Yes, yes I'm ready. What is it?"

I handed her a large note pad and a pencil. "I need someone to sit here and observe and record your observations. Whatever is happening, you write it down."

"But I don't know how to write."

"That's okay," I told her. "Can you draw? Can you give me a few letters that might help me remember what's happening? Like, some signals?"

"Yes! I can totally do that." She grabbed the pencil and I shoved a foot stool over so she could sit and see through the slats into the stall. She settled in, very intent on her job and I smiled.

"Nicely done, Doctor Murphy," came a deep whisper from behind my ear. "You have a way with kids."

I laughed and turned to find him very, very close to me. Lust sprang to life in my core and I desperately wished we were back in my bed.

"Shit," he said. "Do not look at me like that when I can't do a damn thing about it."

I tilted my head. "Oh no? She's occupied." I pushed him back into a door to a storage room right beside Maggie's stall. "We'll be right back, Miller, okay? Just keep observing."

"Got it, Doctor. I'll be okay."

I shut the door and found myself being flipped with my back up against it in an instant. "Rex," I sighed out.

"God, I love it when you say my name like that." He nuzzled my neck and I struggled to keep quiet. There was no such thing as privacy in this barn. The rooms were just slats of wood. Nothing keeping the sounds of pleasure from the outside.

His busy hands slipped into my stretchy jeans, then dipped below my panties, sliding home as I dug my own hand down the front of his pants while my other hand held on for dear life.

"Missed you," he said as he worked his magical mouth up to my ear, where he nipped the lobe, making the ground move a little from the resulting surge of energy coming from my core.

"You just saw me a few hours ago."

"Mmm," was his only response as he slid a second finger inside me. I moved the heel of my hand down his length, remembering how it felt to have him fully-seated inside me. "Come on, angel. Let go for me. But quietly please."

He began to rub my clit with his thumb and I resisted the urge to move with his hand. Not only would I get splinters, but the resulting noise would surely give us away.

"That's it, baby."

My free hand began to roam under his shirt, looking for something to hold on to. When it only found muscle, it gave up the hunt and latched itself onto his spectacular ass and held on for dear life.

"Rex?"

He was administering soft kisses to my chin. "Yes?" He continued on his way, making me struggle to remember what it was I wanted to ask him.

"I—"

"Stop thinking, Ashlyn and let go or we'll be in here all day. Close your eyes and just be. Let it come for you."

"Okay," I whispered back. I did as I was told and felt the warmth moving through my core, rushing towards my nerve endings, ready to make me explode. I frantically grabbed at his ass and my other hand left what it was doing to grab a hold of his hip as I came with one of the most powerful orgasms I'd ever had.

His mouth descended on mine, swallowing my soft cries and it took all of my energy to not shout loud enough to wake the neighbours. I rode his fingers until the wave of extreme pleasure finally began to subside. I opened my eyes to find his beautiful blue eyes smugly looking back at me.

"Hi," he said.

"Hey yourself. I cannot believe we just did that. The whole barn probably heard." My face became hot with embarrassment thinking of the possibility that someone had heard us.

"He smiled and tucked a stray hair behind my ear and moved his other hand out from inside my panties. "You, Ashlyn Murphy, are fucking sexy and that was one of the hottest experiences of my life. We should hang out in your barn more often."

I sighed. I could get used to this kind of thing. Orgasms, companionship, fun. It had been a long time since I'd let myself live on the edge like this.

"Doctor Murphy? I need your help," came Miller's cry from behind the door.

Rex smiled. "She's the best cockblocker around and she's all mine." He began to straighten out my hair and clothes while I came back down to earth. "Don't worry," he said. "This isn't over. I believe, Ms. Murphy, you now owe me something."

He threw open the door to find his daughter impatiently waiting in front of it. "Hey Mills. How'd your observing go?"

"It's boring daddy. The mommy horse is just lying there, licking the baby horse. Are we going to do anything else today?"

"Well, the mommy horse must be pretty tired. And the baby too. Imagine how hard it was moving out of your mom's tummy?"

She took a minute to contemplate that, put her hand on her hip and looked at us like we were the lamest creatures on earth. "I suppose. Can we go now, Daddy?"

"What are you guys up to today?" I asked. God, was there anything more attractive than a super-hot, rough-around-the-edges guy hanging out with his daughter? I felt my ovaries dropping a few dozen eggs while I looked at the two of them.

"Want to come with us, Doctor Murphy?" Miller asked me.

"Oh, well, I don't—"

"Yeah," said Rex. "You should totally come with us."

"I don't know. I should stay and keep an eye on Maggie and I have some clinic hours today. And I could probably use a shower, and well…"

"Daddy doesn't care if you stink," Miller helpfully supplied.

I laughed and discreetly tried to sniff the air around me. Rex sidled up to me, pretending to smell me, and whispered, "Please come. I'd love it if you did."

Well, when he asked nicely. "Okay," I clapped my hands together. "What about this. You give me thirty minutes. I'll find Cam and have him check in on Maggie from time to time, then I'll grab a quick shower in my office. You can either wait for me in the office or wander the grounds. Maybe see what it is we're all about here. I'll check my schedule and see what I can move around."

"Come on, girly. I'll show you my office."

Miller grabbed my offered hand and we made our way through the barn, chatting with the horses and my skeleton weekend crew. I found Cam and asked him to take over Maggie's care and to text me if there were any issues. We finally made it to the second barn and my office/sanctuary.

"Wow!" Miller exclaimed. "This office is not like Daddy's office, at all. This office is so much cooler."

"Thanks! I had it designed as a home away from home. I spend way too much time here in the barns and was tired of sleeping on the hay in the stalls. So, I made this. You're the first two people to ever spend time in here."

Miller ran into the space and flopped down on the inviting couch, Rex settling in beside her. Looking at the two of them, in my very private space, I wondered if I was making the best choices for my heart. This man and this child had the potential to either destroy me or enhance me. I guess it was up to me to make sure the latter, and not the former, happened.

"Alright, I'm going to hop in the shower, then we can go. Actually," I thought out loud, "where are we going? You never said."

"We're going to the movies!" Miller said excitedly. "Daddy's taking the day off and said I could pick any movie I want when we get there."

Ugh, Disney-type movies were so not my thing. Good thing the potential for more sex made up for it. "Okay then. I'll be back in a few minutes."

I quickly showered, changed into some non-horse smelling clothes and we headed out. I managed to avoid Ox, as I wasn't sure he would have followed my wishes and got long gone. He was a problem I was going to have to solve if Rex and I did something long-term with this insane attraction we had for one another.

We hopped in Rex's car and took off for a day of Disney movies and who knew what else. It was the first time I'd played hooky in a while, so whatever happened, I was down for it.

CHAPTER TWENTY-ONE

REX

The week had flown by and I'd managed to avoid my dad and the subject of my dad with Ashlyn. I knew she deserved a long and in-depth conversation about what my intentions were, but if I was being honest with her, I would have only been able to tell her that I had no idea what my intentions were.

I knew my dad wouldn't wait much longer for answers on the property he wanted either. It looked like whatever way you sliced it, I was in for a rocky ride.

I pulled up to Ashlyn's house. It was around seven, so most of the staff should have gone home for the day. I'd either find her in the barns or in her office. Sometimes I wondered why she had such a large home. She was rarely in it.

I decided to check the office first and wandered through the barns, peeking in on the animals as I walked by. I left the first barn and entered the second barn, which was much smaller and only housed a few empty stalls and Ashlyn's office.

I could hear voices at the end of the hall coming from her office, so I quickened my pace as they sounded heated.

"I told you so. I told you this would happen." That sounded a lot like Ox. I hadn't seen much of the arrogant ass who so obviously wanted my girl. He couldn't have her. She was mine. Fuck, I'd become a possessive prick this week. I knew I was falling for her. I couldn't stop myself as hard as I tried. She was the real deal.

Amazing with Miller. A dynamo in bed. Beautiful and considerate and a fucking brainiac. I'd be a fool not to claim her.

"Yes, Ox. I heard you the first fifty times." That was Ashlyn. My only question now was, what in the hell were they talking about? Ashlyn had told me she'd been pissed at Ox and he was currently on a sabbatical from working for her. So why was he now standing in her office, the one place she had never let Ox in before, and why was my girlfriend crying?

Girlfriend. Jesus. That thought just came out of nowhere. I let it settle in and found it kind of fit.

I knocked on the door frame and the two of them simultaneously looked up at me. One with anger and the other with tears streaming down her face. "Ashlyn? What's happened?"

"Get the fuck out of here." This from Ox. Ashlyn still had yet to say anything. She was just standing there, looking at me with tears streaking her mascara. "How dare you fucking show up here after what you've done."

"Wait," I ignored him completely and cautiously stepped into her office. "Ashlyn? What's going on?"

She wiped the tears from her eyes and stood up and walked over to me. "I just have one question."

"Well, that's great, because I have many questions, starting with what the fuck is going on?"

"I lost." That was all she said. She turned and went back to the couch. The same couch we'd laughed on only last week with Miller. The same couch I'd imagined doing dirty, dirty things to her on.

"Lost what? Babe, talk to me."

"I don't want to talk to you, Rex. Please just go." She turned towards the wall and curled up into a ball and suddenly the dots started connecting. This reeked of my father.

"Just tell me what happened and I can fix it."

"That's rich," Ox shouted. "You're going to fix the problem you created. Get the fuck out of here and off this property before I call someone to come and remove you."

"Are you fucking threatening me?" Shit, this was getting out of control, but until I had all the details, there was no way I could fix whatever the hell had happened.

My phone in my pocket started vibrating and as a single parent, I refused to ever let a phone call go to voicemail. I'd never forgive myself if Miller needed me and I ignored the call. I quickly pulled it out and frowned at the number that appeared. My father. He never called me.

I turned and left the office to take the call, giving Ashlyn one last glance over my shoulder, silently pleading with her to just simply look at me.

"Rexford McDaniel," I answered.

"Boy, where in the hell are you? I need you back in the office. Now."

"I can't right now, Dad. I'm in the middle of a negotiation." Well, that was sort of the truth.

"You're going to want to get here now so you can say goodbye to your daughter. Her mother is here to take her back to her home with her. I imagine you're going to want to get here quickly since her flight leaves in a matter of hours."

"You fucking son-of-a-bitch. What have you done?"

The phone went silent and I knew that my whole world was about to implode. From Ashlyn to Miller, it was all over for me. "Ashlyn." She was still refusing to look at me. "I don't know what my father has done, but I promise you, babe, I'll fix this. But right now, I have to get to the office because my ex-wife is here to take my fucking daughter away from me and back to the States. All thanks to dear old dad.

"I'm going to assume he's told you some song and dance about me, my ex and Miller and your property. When I've got Miller back at home, we'll talk. Do not do anything until then. Don't sign those papers. Promise me, baby."

She turned her head to the wall and wouldn't look at me and I was out of time. It always had to be Miller and that reality, right at this moment, fucking sucked.

I ran a hand through my hair and tugged hard enough to feel something other than sheer panic. I walked over to her, placed a soft kiss on her forehead and left to go try to convince my ex-wife to finally do what was in the best interest of her daughter and not take her away for her own selfish financial gain.

* * *

I PEELED into the parking lot, not caring who I nearly killed with my erratic driving. My only thought was hoping that I wasn't too late, which, if I knew my father, was entirely possible. He probably lied to me about the timelines and they were both halfway across the world by now.

I barged into his office, only to find it empty. "Fuck!" I pounded my fist into the wall, barely registering the blinding pain that came after.

"Rex?" Maisie hesitantly peaked into the office.

"What?"

"They left for the private strip about twenty minutes ago."

I hugged her and thanked her and once again found myself tearing out of the parking lot and onto the treacherous Irish highways headed not far down the road to the private airport my father and his associates favored.

I could see a plane on the runway when I pulled in and I sent up a silent prayer that I wasn't too late.

"Dad!" I heard that little voice I'd recognize anywhere as I launched myself out of the car.

"Mills?" I scanned the tiny hanger, trying to find my daughter before it was too late.

"Daddy! Over here!"

I finally saw her just beyond the doors of the hanger, waving her arms at me. "Miller! Angel." I ignored the person holding her hand while I hugged my baby girl. I pulled back and inspected her. "Are you hurt?"

"Oh please," said my ex-wife. "You always were so dramatic. She's perfectly fine."

"No thanks to you, Angela. As usual, your loving and caring ways are out in full force. What do you actually think you're doing?"

"I thought Miller and I needed to reconnect. A little girl time for Mommy and Miller."

I crossed my arms, so thankful I'd caught them before they'd taken off. "Really? And you need to do that somewhere that requires an airplane? Are you also forgetting that we have a custody agreement? An agreement that states I need to give you express permission to have one on one time with Miller." I grabbed a hold of Miller's hand as Angela released it. I hated that our daughter had to see this. No six-year-old should have to bear the brunt of her parents' inability to stay civil in front of each other.

"Can we go somewhere and talk about this before things get out of control?" I needed to get them as far away from the airport as possible.

Angela crouched down and hugged Miller. "Miller, darling. Could you give Mommy and Daddy a few minutes alone, honey?"

Miller looked from me to her absentee mom and narrowed her eyes. "You two are just going to fight and I don't want you to fight. I want to go on a trip with Mommy, Dad. Why can't you come with us?"

"Remember, Mills? Mommy and Daddy aren't in love anymore. We don't do things together, okay? So, why don't you go see if you can sweettalk the pilot into letting you see the cockpit?"

She ran off in search of the pilot and I grabbed Angela's elbow and steered her back into the privacy of the hanger. "What in the actual fuck do you think you're doing? A vacation? What has my father promised you? You know you don't have an ounce of parental rights?"

"Take your hands off of me. I've been rethinking our custody agreement."

"Oh, darling. It doesn't work that way. You see, that's the nature of a bloody fucking legal agreement. It lasts as long as the agreement lasts. You'd need both parties to want to change the agreement and I can tell you with no amount of uncertainty that I do not want to change the agreement. I couldn't think of a worse idea for our daughter."

Jesus, fucking Christ. I could not believe I was right back where I'd started last year. Every God damn year she came sniffing around for something.

She smiled a smile that got botox-blocked pretty quickly. "Rexford. Come on. You're not going to try and stand in the way of a mother who understands that she's done so many things wrong with her daughter and just wants to start to make up for lost time, now would you?"

"Give me a large break. You don't have a maternal bone in that plastic body of yours. I've raised Miller since birth.

Remember that day, Angela? The day you gave birth and looked at our daughter and then turned to the doctor to see if he could give you a little nip and tuck here and there so all 'evidence' of that 'process' was erased?"

I was livid and unable to stop myself. There was no way I was losing everything today. No fucking way.

"What has he offered you?"

Her feigned shocked look was hysterical if I felt like laughing. "What? Who?"

"My father. What did he promise you? Because I can tell you, whatever it is, it'll come with some pretty serious strings attached to it."

"Your father didn't offer me anything."

I grabbed her arms and held her in place so I could look her right in the eyes. "I know he gave you something, because he told me he was. He's been threatening me to stay in line or else he'd give Miller to you somehow. So, now that I've disobeyed him, I know he's done something and for all that is holy, please fucking tell me so I can fix this.

"The woman I love has been destroyed by him somehow and if you leave here with Miller, I'll chase you to the ends of the earth. You do not want to do this. If you think my father can save you from the misery I'll bring down on you, then you obviously don't know me or him as well as you think you do. So, what's it gonna be, Ange?

"Is the money he promised you worth me destroying your precious career? Your reputation? What. Did. He. Do."

I let go of her arms before I turned into someone I couldn't live with. I saw the flight attendants coming our way and knew my time was almost up. "Please. Don't do this."

If there was any part of this woman who had an ounce of compassion, I needed it to hurry the fuck up and show itself.

"He promised me shares. And an incentive. Financial. And, introductions to people who could get me elected. He

179

said if I had a daughter with me, we could play the single mother angle. He'd finance the run for senate and I'd just have to play the part of doting mother. He promised he'd take care of you so you didn't interfere."

I saw red. A lot of red. And not for the first time, I wondered how in the hell I ever thought I wanted a sliver of love from that man. He was pure fucking evil and the woman in front of me was no better. Our entire marriage and the birth of Miller was orchestrated by my father in order to keep me under his wing. He knew damn well what he was doing when he chose Angela for me. And I was the idiot who thought she wanted me for me, not my money.

And the first woman who's looked beyond what I had to who I was probably wouldn't ever speak to me again. The one woman who had every right to hate me, gave me a chance. And Miller. And here I was. Fighting the same damn fight as always.

I was done. But first, I needed to find out what he had done to Ashlyn.

"Miller?" Angela called. Miller turned to look at us with a skeptical eye. Hell, I didn't even know what her mother was up to. "Come here, please."

She skipped over and I was afraid I was about to be left to pick up the pieces that were always left after her mother let her down.

Angela bent down and grabbed a hold of Miller's hands. "Hey. So, it turns out, Mommy can't take that vacation with you just now. It turns out, that Daddy needs you more than I do, as usual."

Miller's bottom lip began to tremble and I raked my hands through my hair. How many times was she going to have to be disappointed in her parents? Fuck, it broke my heart, but if this meant she was going to firmly stay on Irish soil with me, then I'd deal with the expected fallout.

"Why, Mommy?" A tear escaped and Angela brushed it away. I'd give her credit. She was actually trying to do the right thing for a change. Maybe there was hope for her yet. "You said we were going on an adventure."

"I know, darling, but I just remembered that I have to work tomorrow and it's a very, very busy time for me and you'll just be incredibly bored with me. And, I couldn't take Elsa with us, remember? Daddy said you'd miss her something terrible, so I thought it might be best if you stay here with Elsa and Daddy for a while."

"But—"

"Now, Miller. Stop crying. It's unbecoming."

And OG Angela was back. I was beginning to wonder what alien had temporarily taken over her body. I knew her kind streak wasn't going to last. Poor Miller. She was valiantly trying to rein it in, but she was getting more and more worked up as the seconds ticked by.

Angela pulled her in for what might pass as a hug in her world, but was more of an uncomfortable cheek press, with a shoulder grab. And then she was leaving. Good fucking riddance. Don't let the door hit you on the way out.

I grabbed a hold of Miller's hand and gently turned her away from the plane. She was a mess but would rebound pretty quickly, just as she always did. Elsa was a key part in that, but the problem was, I had one stop I needed to make before we could go home and assess the damage from the day. She'd have to hold it together for a little bit longer.

I got her in her booster seat and silently hugged her tiny body. I was her dad. Her protector, but I'd failed her massively today. I didn't know what to say to make up for that, so I figured when she was ready, she'd start talking and let me have it. Until then, if there was one thing I'd learned about raising a daughter, it was to give them space when they needed it. If I pushed her, she'd only lash out.

So, instead, I decided to push a different woman in my life. I still was no closer to figuring out what my father had gone and done to Ashlyn, but the least I could do was apologize for his actions and see if she would give me a little bit of time to try to fix whatever horrible thing he'd done.

Her phone went right to voice-mail as expected, so I left her a quick message so I could get on the road.

"Ashlyn. It's me. I don't know what my father has done but know that I'm in the middle of trying to fix it. If you could just put your hatred of me on hold for a little bit longer, I'd appreciate it. The last hour has been, well, shit. I almost lost Miller, and I know I've probably lost you, but, well, call me back. Babe, I—"

I ran out of words to say and the big words I was thinking of saying just seemed ridiculous right now. I'd never said them to anyone other than Miller and why I thought starting now was a good idea was beyond me. I'd only known her for a month for Christ's sake. And more than half of that we wanted to murder each other. How could my feelings have escalated that quickly?

"Daddy?" Miller called from the back seat. I sighed with relief. She was talking to me again. My little girl wasn't much for grudge-holding, thank God.

"Yes, angel?"

"Why is Ashlyn hating you?"

"I don't actually know, Mills. Grandpa does though, so before we can go home and see Elsa, we need to make a pit stop to ask him. Is that okay? Can you do this for me? I'm sorry to have to ask."

"But it's important," she finished for me.

"Yes, it's very important. Grandpa has likely done a very bad thing to Doctor Murphy and I need to fix it. If I can."

"You can fix it, Daddy. You can fix anything."

"Thanks, Mills. But I'm not sure I can fix this one."

"Daddy?"

"Yes?"

"Is Doctor Murphy in love with you? Is she going to be my new mommy?"

Ouch. Shit, how in the hell was I supposed to answer that?

"I don't know if she's in love with me, baby. And I don't think she's going to be your new mommy. You already have a mommy."

"Not really. Not like all the kids at school. No one there only has just a daddy. Everyone there has a mommy and my mommy just left me here and flew away. So, do you think Doctor Murphy is interested in being my new mommy?"

I was surprised at how that question tugged at my heart and settled itself in my stomach, and not in the bad way. "The truth is, Mills, I hadn't thought about it, and that's a big responsibility to ask somebody to take on. Especially if they're very angry with Daddy right now. So, why don't we just leave it for now and see what happens?"

"Okay, Daddy."

And that, I guess, was that. She was over her mother leaving and on to the next thing, which right now, looked like some sort of book she had stashed in the seat back cover behind me.

We pulled into the offices that contained my father's corporation. I walked up to Maisie, my assistant, and asked if she could hang with Miller while I terminated my position as both Vice-President of the Irish division and his son.

I didn't bother knocking on his open doorframe. I just walked in unannounced and silently closed the door.

"What did you do this time, Father?"

He glanced up with an irritated look on his face. "What are you doing here? Shouldn't you be out trying to get your child back, or something? I thought you'd be halfway to America by now chasing after her."

I stood there, taking him all in. Really, finally looking at him for what he was worth to me. It had taken me this long, but seeing him sitting there, giving zero fucks that whatever he had just done for financial gain had destroyed three lives in the process... I was done, and with that realization came a sense of calm.

I slowly walked over to his desk and placed my hands on the edge, leaning over him to make sure he could look into my eyes. "I'm going to ask you again. What the fuck, did you offer her?"

He tilted his head and smiled smugly. "I didn't have to offer her anything, Rexford. I just told her the truth."

Anger churned deep in my gut. I couldn't believe I'd spent my life trying to please this piece of shit. "Okay, I'll bite. What truth might that be?"

"That the only reason you were sleeping with her was to ensure she sold to us and that you were just doing what I'd asked you to do because you were loyal to me and only me. Family is everything to you. Even if it wasn't true, all it took to bend her to my will was to plant the seed of doubt, son."

He pushed away from the desk and folded his hands in his lap, gazing at me with only curiosity. "You should know better than to go behind my back Rexford. I'll always find out when you're sleeping with the enemy. I don't know what you thought you could change, but the fact of the matter is, I wanted her land and I got it."

"You son of a bitch. What gives you the right to mess with people's lives? To think you have the right to control my life just because we share DNA?"

The anger I'd been trying to hold at bay came surging up on the wings of a fire-breathing dragon. I stalked around the desk, ready to do battle with the old fucker. I'd suppressed my true nature around him for too long. I leaned back against the desk, crossing my arms over my chest and paused. "So, dad. How much did you offer her? How much did she take? How much are the people I care about worth to you?"

He smiled and I had the urgent desire to physically wipe that smile off his face. "One and a half million. A paltry sum and I would have paid more. The girl willingly gave in, especially after I told her how you were just then headed to reunite with your ex, because, remember, family is everything."

I laughed and scratched the beard I'd let start to grow in. Ashlyn had said she was into beards so I'd thought to give it a try. "Good for you, Dad." He visibly recoiled at the word. The familiarity of it was always something he hated. "I mean, one and a half million is a decent sum to compensate someone for taking away their inheritance. Their legacy. Their dream. Any chance I could take a look at the deal? You know, for old time's sake?"

"I wasn't born yesterday, Rexford. You're not coming anywhere near that deal."

I pushed up and off the desk and turned to leave. I'd realized while, I was staring out beyond him and into the wild Irish countryside, that he wasn't worth this fight. There probably wasn't anything I could do to get Ashlyn out of the contract of sale outside of ripping up the contract and there most likely wasn't much hope for her ever forgiving me. But, while I was staring into the eyes of the man I'd worked for so long to gain his love, I'd realized that blood wasn't always thicker than water. Sometimes found family were the family we were meant to have. Like the woman who right now was probably cursing me with all the lovely words she could find. Probably telling anyone who'd listen what a huge dick I was and what I'd done. Or what she thought I'd done.

She also might just be willing to listen to me too. Maybe, she'd be open to hearing about my side of the story. The story that began with one kind of need for love, and had ended with a whole different love. Because, fuck if I didn't love that woman. And nothing this man could do would change that. Land or no land. I was done.

"Dad?

I opened the door to find Miller patiently waiting on the other side. "Hey, Mills. Ready to go see Elsa?"

"Yes, Daddy." She hopped up into my arms and I firmly parked her on my hip.

I turned to see my dad looking at me with narrowed eyes, probably trying to figure out what my angle was. And that was actually the best revenge I could hope for.

"Bye, Dad. I'll have my lawyers send over my resignation and severance request. I think you'll be pleasantly surprised by what value I can put on our family's legacy."

I shifted Miller higher up on my hip, where she wrapped her arms around my neck and rested her head on my shoulder. I had my little girl back firmly where she belonged. Time to get to work on winning my other girl back.

CHAPTER TWENTY-TWO

ASHLYN

A week had gone by since I'd signed that damn contract. Since the bottom of my world dropped out and I made the hasty decision to sell out to the asshole who was Rexford McDaniel II. It was also a week since I'd seen Rexford McDaniel III, his asshole progeny.

A week since I'd been beating myself up. A week since I'd been ignoring everyone and focused only on my practice. And unfortunately, a week since I'd showered. When you worked in a barn, or a vet clinic around animals all day, and you stank, you kind of blended in.

But I knew it was time. I'd taken the money. I'd sold out. I needed to have that hard conversation with my family who, if I didn't answer the phone soon, would come find me in this state. And the prospect of them descending upon me with their noses out of joint was enough to give myself a big kick in the ass.

Rex had only called once. He'd let me know he'd gotten Miller back before his ex could take her back to the States and that he was going to fix everything. I didn't know how he could fix something that I'd come to terms with. I'd done a lot of soul searching since that day and I knew that it wasn't because of what his dad said that I took the deal.

I now knew everything his dad had said was mostly lies. Except for the part where he had made his son get my land. I knew that going into our relationship. That slipup was on me. Rex had never promised me he was anything else. I knew Miller came first. It could be no other way for him.

I'd been left the farmland when my parents died. Each child got some sort of piece of Ireland, except Keeva. She was the baby and just got cash. Which got me to thinking, if Keeva didn't get property, and she was okay with that, why was I so attached to the land I was struggling to manage?

I was a vet. My passion was horses and fixing animals. It wasn't growing a thriving race horse business. It wasn't farming the extra acres. It wasn't spending my entire life doing those things out of a sense of obligation. So, I had signed.

What the asshole didn't know was that I was intending to tell Rex that I would sell the farm to his dad anyway. But then his father came in told me Rex was only hanging around based on orders from his dad and I had believed him. When all signs were pointing in one direction, you should take the signs as being true. I knew he valued his little family more than anything.

He'd left me a message telling me how his dad had threatened that family. He claimed that his intentions had changed on that one fateful day, but he'd have to forgive me if I didn't jump to believe him. He was right. Miller should be his first priority and she needed her dad and her mom and if getting my land secured all those things for him, then I didn't blame him.

But, damn, I missed him. I tried not to, but I couldn't stop thinking about him. I wasn't sure how I felt about him anymore. There was a tiny moment in time I thought I could see a future with him, but now? Now he was just another asshole man who used me to get what he wanted.

I stepped out of the shower and heard voices shouting through the open windows in my office. Quickly drying off, I grabbed panties and a bra, then threw on an old pair of scrubs that should have found the laundry before I put them on again and quickly ran a brush through my hair, re-tying it back up in a scrunchie.

"Ashlyn Murphy, are you still alive?"

Violet. Damn.

"If I drove all the way down here and you're not nearly dead, I swear on my life, I'll get Nixon to go all undercover ninja on your ass. Shit. Was that a horse patty?"

Keeva too? Ugh, this was just what I didn't need. Yet. I didn't need my sisters descending on me, yet.

There was someone banging on my door and I'd just managed to wrap a towel around myself when it burst open and they all tumbled in. Sam, Keeva and Violet came through first, followed by Gray, who I hadn't seen in forever.

"What are you guys doing here?"

"You're clearly alive." This from Samantha. "And obviously in desperate need of our help. Look at you. You're wearing stained scrubs, there's a suspicious smell in here and I'm willing to bet your hair hasn't been out of that scrunchie for at least a week."

She marched over and grabbed the hem of the scrub top I had just wrestled on and yanked it up.

"Sam! What are you doing?"

"Arms up, Ash. This pity party ends today. We're getting you rip roaring drunk at a pub that is not owned by your brother and then that's it. You're going to cash the damn check and get started with the next chapter of your life."

"Arms up. Don't make me repeat myself again." She

sounded like was in full-on mom-mode and I would be stupid to argue with her.

"When was the last time you slept at home?" Violet asked.

"Don't want to," came my muffled reply from under the shirt that was being violently ripped from my body.

"Too bad. I don't care if you had the hottest sex of your life on that bed, you're moving back into a real home. This is an office, no matter how hard you try to convince people it's an apartment."

"Vi! Come on."

"You come on. We're serious. We all have better things to do other than pick you up off the floor and dust you off, but we're here. And while we're here, we're going to get shit done. You're moving back into your house, you're burning those scrubs you've apparently been wearing all week, you're doing your hair and goodness gracious, you need to shave. You could braid that armpit hair and no matter what you've heard, that is simply not attractive to anyone other than the most remote granola cruncher on earth."

"Violet Murphy."

"Violet McGregor. I haven't married that beast of a brother of yours yet, Ash. And at the rate he's going, never will. Let's focus on your love life, if you please. Mine can come another time."

"Gray?" I looked to quiet one of the bunch. Surely she would not condone this manhandling.

"Don't, Ash. Do not look at me like that. You know I can't help you when these three are in control. I'm just here for moral support."

"For who?"

"Whoever needs it. But it would be a lot easier if you could just move this along. Aiden's been on call for a week and I need a break. Preferably one that provides you whiskey and me fried food." She pushed her glasses up her nose, crossed her arms and gave me the patented mom stare that I had been trying to avoid from Sam all this time.

There was clearly no hope. I needed to just let them do whatever it was they needed to do in order to make their spouses, who also doubled as my overbearing brothers, feel better.

"Do you have clothes in this place?" Keeva was rooting through my space while Sam had undone my scrubs and pushed my pants down.

"Step out and drop your drawers, Murphy." Sam laughed to herself. "Oh, if I had a dollar for every time I've used that phrase."

"Ew," we all collectively groaned.

She rolled her eyes and threw the panties Keeva had found at me. "Put these on and head back in there and lose the hair. It's out of control. A man would get lost trying to find home base. Get a grip on yourself woman."

I gave up. I truly didn't have the energy to fight with them. At this point, it was easier to just do as they said and wait for tomorrow when they would all return to their spouses. I got down to the business of hair removal and reappeared a good while later with skin that glowed and didn't repulse my sisters.

I caught the clothes that flew at my head when I emerged and scowled. "I'm not wearing this. Where did it even come from? I don't own clothes like this."

"We know. You can't go to the pub in scrubs, Ash. Put it on and we'll get moving. The sun's setting and your fairy Godmothers aren't always able to stay awake anymore. Let's get a move on."

I held up the fabric and winced. There wasn't much to it. "People in Irish pubs don't wear crop tops. This is nuts."

"What do you care what people in Ireland wear? Just put it on. When you're drunk as a skunk, it won't make a lick of difference." This from my bestest friend in the whole wide world and the only one in this room whose idea of sexy was jeans and T-shirt.

"Fine. But know that one day, I'll have my revenge. And then you'll all be sorry."

"Yes, yes. That's just great," Keeva said before she turned me around and pushed me back in the bathroom. "Get in there and put some makeup on, do your hair and let's get you to the drinking part. Hurry on, now. Come on."

I put on the scraps of fabric and looked at myself in my mirror. I was wearing the shortest black denim skirt known to man, and a top that ended just above my breasts, exposing my tummy and the soft curve that led to my hips. If they let me pair it with flats, I just might be able to stay under the radar.

I ran a brush through my hair, dried it a bit with the hair dryer and applied a couple of coats of mascara and lip gloss and went in for a closer look. My eyes looked like they'd been crying all week, so I dug out some concealer, patted it down with setting powder and ran out of time. The yelling from the other side of the door was escalating and it looked like we needed to get gone.

"Finally," Sam said as I walked out. Then silence. The four of them stood there, frozen, just staring at me.

"What! What did I forget?" I asked.

"You look amazing," Gray whispered.

"Wow," Violet said. "We are pretty amazing."

"Here." Sam put some shoes in my hand. "We found these and they're perfect."

Damn, heels. I bent over and slid into the shoes I'd bought months ago for a wedding in Dublin I'd had to go to and hadn't touched since. "Great, guys. Now I'm six feet tall again. I look like a hooker and I'm having severe déjà vu."

"A damn fine one at that," said Sam. "Let's go. Gray's driving."

We all walked through the empty barns. It was late and most of the staff had left for the day. We got in Gray's SUV and it was then I noticed no one else was dressed up. "Hey! Why am I the only one wearing clothes like this?"

"None of us needs to get back in the saddle," said Violet. "That's why. Step on it Gray. I feel the need to let off a serious amount of steam tonight."

My brother was a notorious asshole. An asshole who whole-heartedly loved my best friend. But after they had the twins, he was also incredibly protective of his family and it was driving Vi a little crazy. They'd come to blows soon, then kiss and make up, just like they always did.

We drove past the beauty of Ireland and I lost myself in the magic of the rolling green of this country. I loved it here, but they were right. I couldn't spend the rest of my life sitting in my office, moping about what could have been.

Just when I thought I was good with moving on, we drove past the entrance to McDaniel Farms. My heart suddenly chose that moment to break in two, yet again, and I thought about what Rex and Miller were up to. I continued to torture myself thinking about Elsa and wondering if she was healing okay.

No, I would not let thoughts of them creep in again. Ashlyn 3.0 started tonight. We drove for a few more miles until we came to a popular tourist town not too far from my home. There was a pub we'd all wanted to try there.

We parked, walked in, quickly found a table and got down to the business of drinking and eating.

An hour or so later, Vi, Sam and I were well on our way to obliterating whatever was bothering us. Gray had abstained, since she was pregnant. My brother, the owner of the super sperm was once again in uber-protective mode and it was a miracle she'd been able to escape to come out tonight.

I couldn't blame him. The last time Gray was pregnant, she nearly died and Aiden missed the birth of August. But man, I didn't envy Gray the next seven months. She would be in Aiden jail until this baby was safely delivered.

The waiter dropped off our fifth or sixth round and the DJ started up and I noticed my soul felt a little less heavy. A bass-heavy dance song came on and we all screamed. "I love this song! Ladies? I think we need to dance."

We hopped up and ran to the dance floor. That was best part about being from a big family. Total built-in girl posse. We danced like fools, spinning each other around and around and falling into various people. My sisters, because, let's face it, even though some of them were sisters-in-law, they were my sisters through and through, kept moving me around and then planting me in one spot.

"Stop!" I held out a hand when another came in to grab me and move me. "Stop man-handling me!"

They laughed and had this weird look in their eyes, every one of them. Of course, it could also have been the alcohol. I wasn't a big drinker, so the last round had hit me hard, but I was having a blast forgetting all about Rex.

My eye caught site of a man off to the side and my heart skipped a beat. For a hot second I thought it was him. He was tall, had the same muscular arms and was wearing the hell out of a tight-fitting Henley shirt and blue jeans. But this guy had short hair. Cropped short at the back and sides, and kind of messy and a bit longer on top, a la Chris Hemsworth with short hair.

Shit, I didn't know what to make of it. I needed to find a man who looked the opposite of Rex, then maybe I wouldn't be thinking I saw him every time I saw a guy that looked remotely like him.

Violet lurched into me again, swung me around and then did that weird planting of my feet in one spot again. "Vi," I grabbed her arms. "Please stop spinning me."

She just smiled and winked at me. Jeez, she must really be drunk. I'd never in all the years of being friends with her, seen her wink at anyone. She walked away and I saw why she was winking. The guy that I'd mistaken for Rex had turned around.

"Holy shit."

He was staring right at me, with those deep, intense blue eyes that I would know anywhere. I fucking saw them every time I closed my own eyes.

I looked around to see that I was suddenly completely alone on the dance floor and I sobered almost instantly. He smiled and started walking towards me when I heard it. The intro to my favourite love song from when I was a teen. "Violet," I whispered. "You're so dead."

"Hi," Rex said as he came to stand directly in front of me. Toe to toe, we just stood there while the song began. "Would you like to dance?"

"Your hair. It's gone."

He smiled again. "Yes, it is." He softly picked up my hand that had fallen to my side in his and wrapped his other arm around me, moving me in as close as he could to his warm, strong body.

I was still struck mute, but he began to move us gently in time to the music. I still wasn't able to find my sisters, but if they had left me here alone with him, there would be hell to pay. What was I thinking? Of course they had, those meddling wanna-be matchmakers.

I gave in to his intoxicating smell and the music coursing through me, and leaned in to rest my head on his shoulder. In heels, there weren't a lot of men who I could do that with and if this was the last time I was held by him, I wanted the full experience.

"I'm sorry, Ashlyn," he whispered in my ear. "I'm so fucking sorry."

I lifted my head to look at him, still struck dumb by his lack of hair. "You cut your hair."

He pursed his lips, holding in laughter and I felt his finger trace the outline of my cheek. "God I've missed you," he said.

"Me too." Oh boy. I couldn't believe I'd just admitted to that. Damn me and my weak resolve and the copious amount of alcohol I'd consumed.

He pulled me closer and rested his hand on the curve of my lower back and I went back to resting my head on his shoulder. I desperately had a million questions for him, but I didn't know how to be the one who made the first move. I was Doctor Ashlyn Murphy. Fully in control at all times and never admitted to vulnerability.

But he was here and I was in his arms and it felt so right and I just wanted to give in to that feeling. We had a lot of stuff to talk about before I could do that, but, for now, I gave in to the pull of the music and the feel of his body up against mine.

We stayed this way, swaying and moving with the music, both of us trying to talk to the other with our movement. I had questions. And accusations. And he hopefully had answers. And he still had a great ass that I had to consioucously force my hand not to grab a hold of while we were dancing.

The music ended and the awkward set in. I didn't know what to do with my hands now that the music wasn't playing. "So…" I stuttered out. "What are you doing here?"

He took my hand like it was his place to do so and if I argued he would refuse to listen and pulled me in his wake to the exit. I looked around and frantically tried to find my sisters.

"They're gone. They're at Gray's for the night," he said.

"So I was right. You did plan this." Damn. We weren't starting out on a good foot.

"I didn't plan this, your family did. They had to convince me awfully hard to come here tonight."

He continued to pull me along, out the door and into the cool Irish evening, always in charge. Always expertly commanding the energy around him to obey his wishes, myself included.

"Wait. Where are we going? I don't know what's happening. I don't even know if I want to find out." My head was spinning slightly and I was starting to see multiple Rexes. Oh dear, this wasn't good. "Rex? I don't feel—"

I felt him pick me up behind my knees and carry me effortlessly the remainder of the steps to his car, gently, tenderly placing me on his luxurious front seat. I was terrified of puking all over his leatherwork. Thank God we weren't far from my house. This was becoming a pattern with us.

He buckled me in, smoothed back the hair from my damp forehead and placed a sweet kiss there. "Close your eyes, Ashlyn. I'm taking you home."

I did as I was told and couldn't be sure, but potentially fell asleep with a soft snore coming from my mouth. It had been so long since I'd slept well. My whole world had been turned upside down this week and before that, he'd turned it on its side.

I woke up with the feeling of him lifting me from the car and carrying me inside, laying me down on a very unfamiliar bed. "Where are we? This isn't my house."

"No, babe. It isn't your house. It's mine." Oh God. I lurched up off the bed and met a brick wall of resistance.

"Rest, Ashlyn. You're in no shape to drive and we need to talk. So, just sit back and close your eyes. I've got you."

My eyes followed him around the room as he busied himself with settling in for the night. He disappeared for a bit and I could hear him talking to the dog. I smiled. I missed his nutty dog and Miller. I definitely missed Miller.

I must have closed my eyes again, because the next time I opened them, I was in a T-shirt that wasn't mine, under the covers with Rex softly snoring beside me, lying on top of the covers in a classic Victorian gentlemanly move.

I took a deep breath in and let it all out. He'd left me a large glass of water and two pain pills on the side table. I sat up and swallowed them back, used the bathroom and slipped back into his huge, luxurious bed and tried to calm my nerves.

"You okay?" he asked from the darkness beside me.

"Yes, I'm fine. Thanks for the pills."

He rolled onto his side to face me. "Thanks for not freaking out tonight. Honestly, I didn't know why I agreed with your sisters to meet them there, but I'm really glad I did."

"They can be very persuasive."

"They have ways that the government could use to lure terrorists."

We both broke out laughing. I felt his fingers tentatively slide along my exposed arm and it sent shivers up and down my body.

"I wasn't sleeping with you for your land, Ashlyn."

"I know."

"Do you? Do you really know? We haven't had that much time to spend together getting to know each other. It's funny..." he paused. "I was on my way to see you that day to deliver a grand speech I'd practiced all the way there. I was going to tell you all about my father and his threat to take Miller away from me if I didn't get you to sell us your land."

"Oh? Yeah?"

His finger travelled up farther towards my shoulder and I shuddered. "Yeah, I was. And then, well, you know what happened next. I was too late. My dad had already put his plan into motion and I lost you and nearly lost Miller too."

"Is she here? Miller?"

"No, she's at Maisie's house. For the entire weekend."

"Confident, aren't you?"

He chuckled and I could picture his eyes crinkling and that rugged, masculine face welcoming me home. The dark was proving to be good for us tonight. Somehow not being able to see him fully was awakening the other senses I had and allowing the vulnerability in. His touch was stirring something inside me. His voice, resonating deep in my core and hell, he always smelled so damn good that it was hard to resist burrowing into his chest just to smell him. And the thought of tasting him was taking over every other thought inside my head.

"I love you." His words washed over me and lit me up, turning my heart inside out. "I left the company, took my father to task and am in the process of taking him for a financial ride. I solidified my position with my ex. Miller is mine, fully. And now all that's left is you."

"You cut your hair off." Man, I was still stuck on simple sentences.

"I did."

"What does Miller think of it?"

"Says I have the same hair as the dog now."

I burst out laughing and he joined me. Before I knew it, he'd scooped me up, shifted me over and stretched out over top of me. I reached out to feel his hair. "It's so short."

"It was time. I had to let it all go. Every damn thing I'd

been doing to get something from my father, including the damn hair." His breath mingled with mine, his lips were so close. "I love you, Doctor Ashlyn Murphy. It's fast, it's nuts, but it's me. You have all of me."

I didn't know how to answer him except to slowly close the inch of space that was left between us and softly taste him.

His lips crashed into mine along with his body that he'd been holding above me. We frantically clawed at each other, neither willing to slow down or give up control to the other one.

"God I was such an idiot. I can't believe I thought giving you space was what I needed to do." His mouth was trailing a path down my neck, heading towards the bottom of the T-shirt I wore. He tugged the shirt up and I sat up so he could get it off me as fast as possible.

I laid my hands on his chest and it was then that I realized he was miles ahead of me in the clothing department. "You're naked already."

"I'm a master, sweet cheeks."

"Hmm," I said. "Prove it."

He gently smacked my rear end. "Minx. Fuck, I've missed you. Have I said that yet?"

I reached up and pulled his head up to my mouth again. "No more talking. Talk later."

"Yes ma'am."

He reached beyond me over to the side table and opened up a drawer, pulling out a small square foil packet. "Hurry, Rex."

He sat back on his heels, put the condom on in record time and settled in between my open legs. I bit down on my lower lip in anticipation and he grinned. "Hey, babe."

I raised an eyebrow to move him along. We'd do sappy after.

He surged in and I sighed. Wrapping my legs around him, urging him deeper, and at the same time arching my back up off the bed.

No words were spoken. Just hot, sweaty sex. Quick, driving thrusts that I could feel to my core. We'd almost missed out on this and we had a lot to make up for. This time would be for those sleepless frustrating nights. The nights we both didn't know how we'd gone wrong or how we'd fix things.

He moved a hand to brush up against my clit and a thousand bolts of electricity shot through me making me cry out.

"Come on, baby. Come for me."

A few more flicks of his talented fingers and I did just that, arching off the bed, forgetting who I was and probably speaking in tongues. He quickly followed me into the abyss of orgasm and then dropped back down to hover over me again.

"Hi."

"Hi," I replied. "I love you too."

"I know. Now, you up for round two?"

"*Miller? You in here?*"

I'd been looking for her for ages and I was beginning to panic. Rex and Miller had moved into my house only a few weeks ago and that girl was always disappearing on us. There were so many opportunities for mischief that I could see the allure, but today was different. Today was my wedding day and I was worried she would be hiding instead of playing.

I opened the door to my office and checked there to make sure she wasn't playing around in here like she usually was. It was in the silent moment before I left that I heard it. I heard the soft sound of a small voice.

I quietly followed the sound until I found the source. She was in the stall that was now occupied by Princess Anna. After I sold the land to Rex's father, I left the horse business altogether and really didn't want to continue breeding and racing and so I sold a lot of my stock. But I gifted Miller the foal she'd helped bring into the world, and she promptly named her Princess Anna. Elsa the lab's newest sister.

I didn't know whether or not to intrude on their conversation. The three of them had become thick as thieves. Miller spent all her free time with her two pets and it looked like she was settling her nerves with her posse again this morning.

"I'm finally getting a mommy guys. I mean, I have a mother, but she's not a mommy. She's just a mean lady who gave birth to me. Ashlyn is a real mommy. Elsa, you're gonna love her even more as our momma. You can get into all the trouble you want now. We've got a doctor to fix you."

Oh my freaking heart. If it was possible to melt from emotion, today was surely going to liquify me.

"We've got a lot to teach her, of course, but she's pretty awesome. And Daddy really thinks she's great. He even cut all his hair off for her. And he loves her and they're always kissing and touching each other in weird 'tickle' places. I don't get it, but, hey, what can I do?"

I smiled and couldn't stand outside any longer. I needed to hug this little miracle.

"Miller?"

"Oh, hi Ashlyn. Are we ready to get married?"

"We are. Are you ready?" I looked her over. She had some hay stuck to her hair and dress, but for the most part, she would do. "Your dad and everyone is waiting for us. We've got a bit of a drive to Murphys. We really should get going."

She hopped up and grabbed a hold of my hand. "Bye Elsa. Bye Anna. Be good." She squeezed my hand and smiled up at me. "Ashlyn?"

"Yes, Miller?"

"When can I start calling you Mommy?"

I knelt down and looked her in the eyes. "Whenever you're ready."

"Okay, Mommy. I'm ready."

I looked up to see Rex standing there in his tux, looking at us with such love in his eyes. It'd been almost a year since we'd met and we'd only been living together for a few months, but this man and his daughter were my everything.

"She called you mommy," he whispered in my ear.

I wasn't sure I could grin any harder. "I know," I whispered back.

"Ready girls?" He held open the doors of the car and we slid in the back, Rex driving up front. We were staying in Castlegregory, just down the road from the church and Murphy's Pub. Miller would be staying with Sam and Brennan while we honeymooned for a couple of nights on our own, then the three of us would take off for a trip to Disneyworld. Completely unconventional, but this was the family I'd always dreamed of and hanging with them in Disney seemed pretty perfect.

"Ready!"

* * *

WE STOOD TOGETHER at the edge of the world, me in my wedding dress and Rex in his tux, holding hands, my head resting on his shoulder as I looked out over Brandon Bay. This was where I'd grown up every summer. My mother having been born and raised here and who had brought us home every school summer break to work at the pub, swim in the ocean and find our Irish roots.

Behind us, the pub was alive with dancing and celebrating as only the Irish knew how to do, but out here, there was only the two of us. Miller had left to go stay with her cousins and it was soon time for us to head to our rented rooms down the road.

Rex turned me to face him while the wind whipped my hair all around us. He took a hold of my face, placing his hands on my cheeks and resting his forehead against mine.

He'd never let his hair grow long again, so it was only mine that was out of control out in the elements.

"I love you," he whispered into the wind. He turned his head to look back at the pub and laughed to himself. "Imagine a kid growing up desperate for anyone else to stand beside him. A family that consisted of more than an absent, money and power-hungry father and a mother who only gave birth to you out of duty. And now look at this. Look at this family you've given me."

"Are you sure you want them?" I said as a particularly rowdy yell barreled through the doors. "They are often a real pain in the ass."

"I want all of it. The fights, the partnerships, the laughter, the love. I want Miller and our children to grow up surrounded by family. I want you and everything that comes with you."

He turned back to me and gathered me up in one of his spectacular bear hugs. The setting sun took a hold of our hearts as it disappeared over the edge of the surrounding cliffs and I could feel the magic of Ireland surrounding us as we began our journey as husband and wife. Doctor Ashlyn Murphy and Mr. Rexford McDaniel III. 'Til death do us part.

The End

Irish proverb
May you always have
Walls for the winds,
A roof for the rain,
Tea beside the fire,
Laughter to cheer you,

Those you love near you,
And all your heart might desire.
May joy and peace surround you,
Contentment latch your door,
And happiness be with you now,
And bless you evermore.

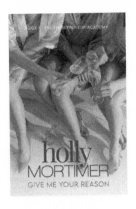

Chapter One

I pulled into the driveway on autopilot and put the van in park. I was pretty sure mine was the only minivan in the Hollywood Hills that wasn't trying to look like an SUV, and that fact always made me snicker to myself whenever I parked.

I pushed the remote for the garage door, pulled in, and shut the car off. Still I stayed put. I did not want to go inside just yet. I wasn't sure I wouldn't lose my mind and yell at my one remaining son living at home, but that was just an excuse I was trying to sell myself.

I was tired. Tired of single parenting four nearly grown men. Tired of running one of the largest, most well-known corporations in America, and tired of swimming upstream as a forty-five-year-old female, award-winning female screen-writer in a world of non-award-winning male screenwriters, and lately I was spending more and more time in the garage and less time walking into my house and dealing with what was practically shouting at me.

I was alone.

Totally alone.

Well, not totally alone in the sense that there would be no one to call if one day I found myself in the unfortunate position of having to give an ER nurse my "in case of emergency" contact person, although when I thought about that, maybe I was right. Maybe I was truly alone.

I leaned my head on the steering wheel and wondered when I'd become the sad, lonely divorcée who couldn't seem to move on after ten years of singlehood. The mom who hid in her garage so her kids couldn't start pelting her with their needs and demands.

A knock on the window had me screaming in fright, and I looked up to find my baby, who wasn't really a baby, but a seventeen-year-old man-child, smiling back at me.

"Mom?" he asked. "You okay?"

I removed the keys from the ignition and grabbed my backpack from the passenger seat. "Yeah, I'm okay, Tom. What are you doing out here?"

He looked at me like he didn't believe me, and I would have agreed with him if given the chance. I didn't believe me, either. "Aunt Poppy is looking for you. She's been trying to call you, but your phone must be off because it wouldn't pick up. So, she texted me and told me to go check the garage before I called the police."

I got out of the car and air-kissed his cheek as he reared back, trying his best to escape my mothering like a good teenager. "I'll call her later. Thanks for not calling the police."

"Yeah well, you do spend a lot of time in the garage when you get home, you know, preparing yourself or whatever it is you do out here."

"Huh," I muttered to myself. Just what I needed. A kid who paid too much attention to me. "Come on, bug." I tried to put my arm around him, but he scooted under me and ran into the house. "I'm starving. Let's find something to eat."

I dropped my backpack on the kitchen floor, leaned against the counter and took a deep breath, surveying the state of my kitchen.

The dishes on the counter indicated he'd eaten at least three times since coming home from school so I wouldn't have to rush.

Out of the four boys I'd raised practically on my own, Tom was the biggest eater. He had a tapeworm permanently living in his stomach. I was sure of it. He just ate and ate and never gained any weight, the poor kid. Well, he hated it, but I envied him his lightning-quick metabolism.

At forty-five, I was sliding downhill toward the dreaded fifty and there wasn't anything left inside of me resembling my youth.

Pooch over my C-section scar, dimples on my butt and thighs, sagging and spreading boobs, and stretch marks for days on my hips. Oh, the metabolism of a perimenopausal woman. If that didn't add up to something spectacular, I didn't know what did.

Four boys all at least a foot taller did something to you. It was constant motion, it was anger and passion, it was the catching something to eat on the way to various sporting activities. Early mornings on the field and late nights worrying if they were being smart. It all added up to who I was today.

Sure, I was the CCO of the most powerful animation studio around. Sure, I directed Academy award-winning films, and sure, I wrote a lot of the stories children and their parents deeply loved. But my boys had almost all grown and flown. The closest thing I'd gotten to a dating life was that weird screening we'd had at a senior's center last year and I'd stayed to celebrate a member's one-hundredth birthday and gotten a kiss on the cheek for my time.

It was official. I was doomed.

I grabbed my phone and saw that Tom was right. Poppy had attempted to reach me in every way possible. She must have really needed to talk to me to use Tom as her conduit. I didn't even know they had each other's numbers.

I called her, put her on speaker, and moved through the silent house to change before finding my corner of the couch and vegging out to a show on Netflix everyone but me had seen. Poppy was one of my circle of six. It sounded like a cult, but the truth was just a group of like-minded women, all high relators and number one achievers on the Gallup scale.

I had been asked to join a group of women who were considering starting their own businesses and, thinking it would be a good way to meet new people who weren't looking for an appearance at their kids' next birthday party, I had agreed to become the lead mentor at the Entrepreneur Academy.

I was pleasantly surprised when I actually did connect deeply with the five women who were my mentees. Poppy was in PR and had been building her own firm on the side ever since I'd known her. She and I had hit it off with our mutual hatred of a few people we both knew. Nothing like a good friendship built on substance I always said.

Last month she'd finally managed to walk out of the firm where she was treated like a number, not a human, and she'd managed to take a couple of high profile clients with her. She'd been calling me every day in a panic that she was about to fail and fail spectacularly. She'd probably had another run-in with her ex. The same ex who happened to own the company she used to work for.

"Hello?" She sounded like she was standing in the middle of traffic. "Clem?"

"Pops. Where are you?" I ran up the stairs and headed into my closet to shed my bra and throw on my comfiest track pants. "It sounds like you're standing on the freeway."

"Ugh, I'm at a party and it's jam-packed. Hang on, I'm going to find a quiet room. Fingers crossed it isn't occupied."

"Ew," I said as I set the phone down and quickly stripped and redressed. I grabbed a hair tie, pulled up my hair, and set back off downstairs to see what I could scrounge up for dinner.

"Okay, Clem. You there?"

"I'm here. What's up?" I grabbed a pack of chicken fingers and some fries and got to work preparing my go-to, I'm too exhausted to cook, meal. It was my version of comfort food and I had had a long day. At least I'd gotten organic chicken fingers so I could pretend it was healthy.

"So, I need a favor."

In my experience, I need a favor was usually followed by something I would regret agreeing to. "Okay, what?"

"Remember when you said last week how much you missed the snow? And how you'd love some time just to be still and get out those words that had been stuck somewhere inside you?"

"Out with it." I was a no-bullshit kind of person. Total straight-shooter and I couldn't stand it when someone beat around the bush. "Poppy, just ask me. You know I won't say yes unless I want to."

"I need someone to babysit a client. And, well, I think that someone should be you."

"What? My babysitting days are over. Hire the kid a nanny or something."

"He's forty years old. He might not take kindly to a nanny."

"Jesus, Poppy. I'm not babysitting Rhett Montgomery." No way, no how.

"Why do you think it's Rhett?"

"Please. I know your roster and he's the only one on it that could have gotten himself in enough publicity trouble for you to ask me, the last person on earth who is kind to someone needing a second chance. It could only be him."

"Well, okay, yeah, it's Rhett. Please, Clem? I'm throwing in my condo in Whistler for a week."

Jeez, she must be desperate if she's getting him out of the country altogether. "After the favor or that's where the favor is taking place?"

"I need him far away for a few days while I take care of a few things he's gotten himself into."

"Like what? What things could that man possibly have done that's so bad he needs to leave the country?"

Rhett and I had a volatile history. He was obnoxious, egotistical, and all the other words you could think of that described the Playboy of the Century, as he'd been named last year by all the magazines. He'd cornered me once at a launch party that Poppy had convinced us all to go to.

I might run with that crowd on a day-to-day basis at work, but my personal time was blessedly ego-free. That night he'd decided I was going to fall head over heels in love with him. I had a few rules. No relationships ever with people I worked with or might be working with in the future, and he'd just auditioned for a role in a film I was directing. But larger than that, I didn't date celebrities. There were usually more than two people in the relationship. Me, them, and their ego. Been there, done that, have the ex-husband to prove it.

"I can't say, just that it's all bullshit. He needs to lay low, but there's too much stuff going on here and he's likely to just get into something while I'm trying to sort out this mess. I know you love going to Whistler and it's January and snowing and the village will be all snow-covered and beautiful, just like you like it.

"You don't have to talk to him, or even see him once you're there. There're two bedrooms, so he'll probably stay in his room and you in yours. The plane ticket's on him. You'll fly private. Come on, what do you think?"

She took a breath, and I gave my head a shake for momentarily getting sucked into her sales pitch.

"You know you never take a break and you've got the time, Clem. You're in the middle of production, you said so yourself. You've got some breathing room. And, oh, you could finish up the rewrites. Also, you can't tell anyone where you are, if you don't mind."

"Oh, if I don't mind? Poppy, I have children. They need to know where I am at all times."

"So, you'll do it?"

"What? Wait, I never said—"

"Oh Clem, I owe you big time. I've got to run. Rhett isn't too happy about the plan but now that he knows you're going with him, he'll be totally in."

"Poppy! I never—"

There was silence on the other end, and I didn't exactly know what to do at that moment. She'd railroaded me into being a willing participant in her scheme and I was so discombobulated I wasn't sure if I was actually going or if I was going to call her back and make sure she knew I wasn't going.

My phone chimed with an incoming text as I was sitting there debating my next move. Thinking it was Poppy, I unlocked it and saw it was from my youngest child. Ugh, I was such an enabler. I couldn't ever get mad at that kid, even when he texted me questions from his room.

What's for dinner?

I rolled my eyes and instantly texted back, knowing I

wasn't doing anything for that missing communication bridge my son and I needed to build.

Chicken fingers

Again?

Would you like to make dinner?

I watched those three moving dots dance around the screen for a few seconds and smiled despite the heaviness I was currently feeling. I knew him. If he had a better idea, he would have made it himself ages ago. Hell, he probably had already eaten an entire loaf of bread when he had gotten home from school and was just now getting hungry again. He would hold on the offer to cook dinner.

My phone chimed another incoming text, and I debated about starting to curb my addiction to the damn thing. *Ugh,* was my internal reaction when I unlocked my phone and saw it was my ex who had texted me.

Not that I hated him, or thought he was awful, it was just when I needed to sort out a problem that was plaguing me, I needed zero distractions and he was a distraction. He struggled to remember we were divorced sometimes. Immediate responses were about all he would expect.

I took my chances and decided to ignore it and move on with my most pressing problem. I started texting Poppy back, while leaning on the kitchen counter staring out at my expansive backyard. The backyard that sold us on this incredible house. The one with the pool and the grassy area and the privacy. The yard that was perfect to raise a family in. Now, I stood there absently thinking and staring at the empty yard.

I heard Tom practically falling down the stairs and braced for impact, letting my phone and text stay open at *'Pops, this isn't...'*

"Dinner ready yet?" He predictably asked.

"I just put it in five minutes ago."

"Okay, calm down. I was just asking."

"Um, I don't feel like I was yelling?"

He rolled his eyes and sat down to alternately stare at the oven and his phone. I busied myself with tidying while I debated about how I was going to handle the Poppy and Rhett situation.

"Tom?" I asked before I could talk myself out of it.

"Yeah," he replied without even looking up from his phone. A skill I was positive most teenagers received magically on their thirteenth birthday.

"You're at your dad's next week, right?"

"Yes." Still hadn't looked at me, so it was now or never.

"I need to head out of town for the week. Can you take Ripley with you? You okay with that?" Wait, what? How had I changed my mind in the last two minutes without even realizing it? Ripley, our yellow Lab looked up at me and I swore he was smiling.

"Sure." His one-word answers were getting on my nerves.

"Do you not want to know where I'm going?"

"I don't know. Something for work?" He finally looked up at me like there would never be another possibility so why was I acting so weird?

"Well, it's not something for work. I'm helping out a friend of Poppy's and I'll be heading up to Whistler."

My kids were very familiar with Whistler. Since I loved it there, they loved it there. Their dad and I used to take them skiing there every year when they were little and I'd tried to keep it up, although I wasn't very good at it. I loved Whistler. But I didn't ski. Every ski vacation was just me waiting for everyone to be done skiing. I was terrified of the sport and it was a huge fight each year with my ex just to get me to agree to let the kids fly down the side of a deadly mountain on two sticks.

The stunning scenery won me over every time and the

kids had taken to skis like they were born to it, so who was I to argue? I just went along with it as per usual. Now that their dad and I had split, I tried to continue our traditions, but they more often went with him.

"Whistler?" he asked. "You hate it there."

"I don't."

"Do, too. You only went 'cause Dad wanted to."

"Well, for your information, I happen to love it there, I just don't love to ski. Maybe this time I'll take a lesson." Fat chance, but this was another moment I was becoming aware of how my kids saw me, and if what I was thinking was right, they didn't always think I had been able to stand my ground when their dad and I were married.

He snickered and I ignored him, turning to get the chicken fingers out of the oven, feeling the sting of tears that rarely fell hitting the back of my eyes. What the hell? I didn't cry. It wasn't my jam. Damn perimenopause. Fucking hormones making a comeback this late in life was such a crock of shit.

"Thanks, Mom," he said as he grabbed his plate and took off to go back to his room and I decided there and then that I was going to Whistler and I would use the opportunity to elevate my status in this family.

I grabbed my phone and shot Poppy a text, very different than the one I was originally intending.

Tell me more.

I just chartered a plane. It will pick you up tomorrow at the Sinclair airfield outside of town at 10:30. You'll land at a private airport in Vancouver at three-thirty. I've rented you a car with a nav system pre-programmed. Just follow the route to the condo. It's a coded entry. Code is 81761. It's a two-bedroom. Yours is walk-out, his is top floor.

Anything else I should know? Like what the hell he did to have to run to Canada?

That's his story to tell. If you read the entertainment news like a normal human, you'll know by the morning. Thanks, Clemmie. I owe you huge.

Why does he need a babysitter? He's a grown man. Is there something you're not telling me? I don't have time or the interest in the entertainment news. He's not an ax murderer, is he? Have I done something to you I'm not aware of?

NO! I just don't trust him not to interfere with my work while I'm cleaning his mess up. He needs someone with him who, well, who will make sure he stays inside, sober, and working. His agent said he's got some critical auditions in a few weeks he needs to be ready for. He can't be out partying in Whistler, Clem. Promise me you can do this. He's my biggest client and without him, my business will sink.

So, in other words. I'm supposed to act like his mommy and I'm the least exciting person you know, sooooo...

Whatever you do, she carried on choosing not to respond to my text, *do NOT sleep with him.*

OMG Poppy. Ew.

Well you know he had that weird thing for you a couple of years ago. And he can be very persuasive. That's how we got into this mess. Look at him. He's practically irresistible.

I'm well aware of his finer qualities and I'm pretty sure you're well aware of my rules.

That's why I thought of you right away. You're the best rule follower around.

A slight pang hit my stomach and I ruthlessly shut it down. I was a rule follower. You had to be when you were the boss of a large company. I got shit done and I got it done right and that wasn't because I did anything other than work and follow the rules—society's and my own.

Yeah, and look where that's gotten you, that little inside voice whispered. *Relentlessly single with a best friend who picked you to play the part of the stern governess.* That didn't scream "able to live life to the fullest."

I dropped my phone and beaned the passing cat on the head. She screeched and bolted, and I used the distraction to try to find my focus. Poppy wanted me to babysit only the most beloved actor in America today.

Around forty, large, he was close to six and a half feet tall. Dark curling hair with just the sexiest hint of gray depending on the role he was playing. Rough around the edges. Preferred jeans and a t-shirt to anything trending.

I needed more info. Because, you know, this whole idea was INSANE. I opened my laptop to Google Rhett Montgomery. I was sadly out of touch with pop culture and the entertainment news. Poppy considered E-News to be the equivalent to CNN in her world and at this point, as I was unbelievably accepting her proposal, I kind of wished I had kept on top of her version of the news.

My screen flooded with the latest scandalous news stories from Crazy town. That's what I called LA because as far as I could tell it only made people nuts.

I scanned the headlines talking about his various cheating scandals, his apparent drinking problem, and his inability to keep his hands to himself when out in public. He was said to have been in a long-term relationship with another A-lister I had only kind of heard of. I assumed something had happened that was about to go very public with said A-lister.

This kind of stuff usually blew over after a week or so. I wasn't sure why Poppy was freaking out so hard. Well, I knew why she was. She'd only recently had the guts to go out on her own and Rhett was her first client who paid the bills and could bring in referrals. If she could handle a man who had the PR issues he did, she could probably handle any celebrity. She needed this to blow over as quickly as possible and as her mentor from the Entrepreneur Academy this was the least I could do.

I could use a little time away and being forced to hole up in Poppy's condo on the mountainside was the perfect place for me to get a ton of work done. I had been in a massive writing slump. The words were stuck, and I needed them unstuck before the end of the month so I could keep the production schedule on track.

I texted my assistant, who I knew would get started on rearranging my entire life for me, even though I had told her a million times that when she left the office, she was to ignore me until she got in the next day. Nothing I would need would be life or death important. That is, until today.

End of Sample
To continue reading, be sure to pick up Give Me Your Reason at your favorite retailer.

ALSO BY HOLLY MORTIMER

The Murphy Series

(Contemporary Romance)

Worlds Apart (Book 1)

Expectation (Book 2)

Hacked (Book 3)

Freedom (Book 4)

Undone (Book 5)

Avow (Novella)

.

The Entrepreneur Academy

(Contemporary Romance)

Give Me Your Reason (Book 1)

.

Other Stories

Ignite (Romantic Suspense)

ABOUT THE AUTHOR

Travel romance writer, Holly Mortimer, will transport you to the shores of romantic Ireland, where you'll lose yourself inside the drama and the love that is The Murphy family. From oldest to youngest, these five siblings fall in and out of love, travel the Irish countryside and learn that loving someone, doesn't always go as planned.

Holly transports the reader into her world, filled with travel, babies and lots of alphas!

hollymortimer.com